PLATO
AT
SCRATCH
DANIEL'S

PLATO
AT
SCRATCH
DANIEL'S
AND
OTHER
STORIES

EDWARD
FALCO

The University of Arkansas Press

Fayetteville   London   1990

Designer: Chiquita Babb
Typeface: Linotron 202 Baskerville, with Trajanus

The paper used in this publication meets the minimum
requirements of the American National Standard for Permanence
of Paper for Printed Library Materials z39.48-1984. ∞

Stories in *Plato at Scratch Daniel's and Other Stories* have been
published by the following journals: "Gifts," in *Missouri Review;*
"Prodigies," in *Virginia Quarterly Review;* "The Foaling Man," in
Virginia Quarterly Review; "Silver Dollars," in *Greensboro Review;*
"Peace, Brother," in *Shenandoah;* "This World That World," in
St. Andrews Review; "Something New, Something Diferent," in
Gettysburg Review (Originally published as "Leaning into the
Circle"); "The Girl at the Window," in *Sou'wester;* "Heart Attacks,"
in *River Styx;* "Sir Thomas More in the Hall of Languages," in
Georgia Review; "St. Augustine on MONY Tower," in *Akros Review;*
"Plato at Scratch Daniel's," in *Virginia Quarterly Review.* "This
World That World" was awarded the Mishima Prize from the
St. Andrews Review. "Plato at Scratch Daniel's" was awarded the
Emily Clark Balch Prize from the *Virginia Quarterly Review.*

Library of Congress Cataloging-in-Publication Data

Falco, Edward.
    Plato at Scratch Daniel's and other stories / by
  Edward Falco.
      p.   cm.
    ISBN 1-55728-156-4 (alk. paper). — ISBN 1-55728-157-2
  (pbk. : alk. paper)
      I. Title.
  PS3556.A367P55   1990
  813'.54—dc20   89-29120
                                                     CIP

for
Susan

CONTENTS

PLATO
AT
SCRATCH
DANIEL'S
AND
OTHER
STORIES

GIFTS

---

for
Raoul Vezina
and
Jay Walter

Storm-blue clouds, a circle of slate-blue mountains, a ridge I could barely make out between the mountains and the clouds—that's what it looked like from the bedroom window. The storm winds had entered my dreams as wolves and a woman screaming, and I was relieved when I woke and heard the wind slapping against the cabin walls. For a long time I lay in bed looking at the slow-moving clouds and the leaves rushing through the little alley of cleared land between my window and a hillside that fell off into a long, wide, thickly wooded ravine. I smelled coffee brewing in the kitchen and the smell was rich and enticing, but the bed was warm and the room cold, and I huddled down under the covers and pressed my head into the pillow.

A week before, our house had burned. Ellie and I lost most of what we owned, but we were thankful for our lives, and so I worked things out with the court and my clients and my partners and took two weeks off from being a lawyer so I could take this vacation at Howard's cabin. Actually, it's our cabin: Howard willed it to us when he died. Howard was our son. He was twenty-six when he died six years ago, and since then we've only been to the cabin twice, both times in the last year. It's situated on a little peninsula of land that juts out into a ravine, and it's not a very valuable piece of property because it won't be around much longer: the land it rests on is slowly eroding. In another ten years the cabin will sit on the edge of the ravine, and in another twenty it'll be gone. But the view . . . The view is magnificent. More so now than when Howard was alive.

The first time we saw the place was 1969. Those were hard years. The world was changing before my eyes, and I didn't like what I was seeing. Howard did, and we were always at odds. In college he let his hair grow long, and he came home for holidays with hair like a girl's reaching down to his shoulders. I tried not to look at him. I tried to tell myself it was a fad. He always had a delicately handsome face, and then with that long hair he looked so feminine, he looked so much like a girl that I wanted to smack him and make him get his hair cut. I can still hear myself yelling at him, telling him to act like a man. He was full of ideals—and all I could see was long hair, and a face that seemed too pretty.

But 1969. That spring he had graduated from college and with money he had borrowed for grad school he bought this cabin. We found out not from Howard—we had given up trying to keep track of him—but from his girlfriend's father. His girlfriend's name was T. J., and though he had been seeing her for a couple of years, we had never met her. One night that summer her father called and threatened to shoot Howard if he didn't send T. J. home. After I got him calmed down, he told me about the cabin; and I promised I'd go up there and talk to Howard. By the end of the phone call, though I don't think my voice showed it, I was angrier than T. J.'s father, and not about Howard and T. J., but about the way Howard had spent the grad school money—money he had gotten from a loan I cosigned.

I had wanted to go see him alone, but Ellie insisted on coming.

4

"We really should let him know," she said.

I shook my head and glared at the rutted dirt road. This was not the kind of driving my Buick had been designed for, and every time a rock clunked against the frame I cursed the mountains and grew angrier at Howard. "How?" I said, trying to sound even-tempered. "How do we let him know we're coming?"

Ellie didn't answer. She turned and looked out the window at trees that crowded the road.

"No phone," I said. "No mail delivery. How am I supposed to let them know?"

Ellie touched her fingertips to her forehead, just above her eyebrows—which is something she always does right before she cries.

"Don't cry, Ellie," I said. But the tears were already falling silently down her cheeks. Ellie is a small, frail woman with a delicate face. I knew we were only a short way from the cabin (T. J.'s father gave good directions), and I didn't want Ellie crying when she saw Howard—so I tried my best to calm her down. By the time we got there she was feeling better. I had agreed to walk the half-mile trail to the cabin first, and then bring Howard back to the car. This, Ellie reasoned, would give T. J. time to straighten out her house before we all arrived. I didn't argue. It still makes me smile to think of how concerned Ellie was that T. J. have enough time to straighten out her house for guests.

I was glad for the half-mile walk. It gave me time to compose myself and rehearse what I wanted to say. The sweet smell of the woods was calming, though I was constantly annoyed at the overhanging branches and the uneven path. I was going to tell Howard about how much Ellie and I had sacrificed for him, and what he owed us: first of all, to live someplace civilized, and then to contribute something to society, to give something back in return for what had been given to him. I remember rehearsing that speech when the path opened onto a clearing and I saw the cabin. It's a big log cabin with a slate roof, and there's one large bay window in the front that brings the morning light into the living room; and there's a little three-step stoop that leads up to the front door. The way I was standing at the edge of that clearing, with my legs and arms so stiff, I must have looked like just another tree, because no one noticed me. The cabin door was open, and I could see in through the living room to the kitchen. Howard was sitting at the kitchen table smoking a pipe, and a much older man—he looked to be in his late forties to early fifties—was sitting across from him. T. J. was sitting on the table between them with her legs crossed and folded under her. Her eyes were closed and her hands were resting palms up on her knees. All three were naked. I stood there a long time taking in this sight: T. J., with her boyish flat chest and skinny body, with her long straight hair that reached down to the table top; the older man, whose face was lost somewhere under a disheveled mop of curling mouse-brown hair and a beard that grew wildly over his face; and my son . . . my son Howard, who, if not for the evidence of his sex, could have been mistaken for a pretty, flat-chested girl with silky, dark hair falling over her shoulders. I had just about decided to turn around and leave before anyone saw me, and to tell Ellie no one was at the cabin, when a huge Chow that had been lying on the cabin floor under the bay window saw me. He was a dopey looking dog with a full ruff of long, silver-gray hair. When he saw me, he jumped right into the window. I'm still surprised it didn't break.

All three naked bodies at the table turned at the same time. The older man stood up, and Howard and T. J. leapt for the Chow, who had regained his bearings and was about to make it out the front door. Howard caught it by the collar and T. J. had it by the tail, and still the thing carried them half way out the door before they managed to pull it back into the kitchen and tie it to a short leash. I could hear Howard explaining over the Chow's barking, "It's okay! It's okay! He's my father!", and then T. J. closed the front door and ran through the living room to the bedroom. The older man—whom I later learned was an ex-lawyer, ex-stock broker, ex-corporate executive named Tom McGuinn—must have left through the back door because I didn't see him again. Then the front door opened and Howard, dressed in a white robe with a black silk rope for a belt, walked across the clearing and joined me.

"I'm sorry you didn't let me know you were coming," he

said. He was looking me in the eyes—something I taught him to do when he was a boy. He said, "I'm sorry about how this must make you feel, Dad."

I nodded.

Howard looked away and we were both silent awhile. Then he started talking casually. "Lieberman loves T. J.," he said. "He's such a big, dumb puppy."

I guessed that Lieberman was the Chow.

"A couple of weeks ago T. J.'s father came busting in the cabin and Lieberman bit him." Howard smiled.

I nodded again.

"He sent you up here, didn't he? T. J.'s father."

I said, "He's threatened to kill you."

"He's told me in person. T. J. says he won't do it."

"That's nice to know. If she were my daughter, I don't think you'd be so lucky." As soon as I said that, I felt like a jerk.

Howard said, "I love T. J.."

"So you let her sit naked in front of another man?"

Howard looked at me defiantly. "I let her sleep with him too. In fact—"

"Shut up," I said. I grabbed his robe and pulled him close. When he didn't resist, I pushed him away and turned and walked down the path, half expecting him to follow. He didn't; and I remember cursing him as I followed the trail. When I got back to the car I told Ellie no one was at the cabin. She looked at me and knew I was lying. "What happened?" she asked. I didn't answer. I started the car and we drove in silence until we found a motel where we could spend the night.

After I carried our suitcases into the room and stretched out on one of a pair of double beds, Ellie asked me again to tell her what had happened. I told her and she kept shaking her head through the whole story. When I finished she asked, "Are you sure about the other man?" I nodded. I hadn't told her what Howard had said, or even that we had argued. I just told her I had been upset with them and had left. She wanted me to go back. "You have to go back," she said. "We can't leave things this way."

I agreed. Ellie had meant for me to go back in the morning, but I was too upset to wait. After the TV news was over, I left her alone in the motel room and drove back to the cabin.

By the time I arrived it was dark. There was no moon that night and as soon as I turned off the lights and stepped out of the car I couldn't see a thing. I held my fingers in front of my eyes and I still couldn't see them. I got the flashlight out of the glove compartment and let its thin beam of light guide my way. The woods were full of strange noises: at one point as I walked along the trail, I must have surprised an owl or some other large bird, because I heard a great, thick flapping of wings from a tree limb only a few feet in front of me. Then, after my heartbeat slowed somewhat, I began to hear an irregular clicking noise, like someone sending Morse code; and as I continued walking the clicking got louder, until, standing once again at the clearing in front of the cabin, I saw T. J. sitting at the kitchen table typing.

I remember how intent she looked at her work. She stared at that typewriter as if it could talk to her, as if she were waiting for a message to come whispered from its innards. Then suddenly, as if she heard what she was listening for, she'd type furiously for a minute or two, and then stop again to listen. I must have watched her there for ten or fifteen minutes. Occasionally she'd rub her nose with a bent forefinger, or pull a long strand of hair across her lips and bite at it—but always she'd return to her listening and typing. Lieberman was sleeping on his back in front of the bay window, and McGuinn was sitting on the couch reading a thick, dark book.

Quietly and carefully, I walked around to the back of the cabin. There, through the bedroom window, I saw something that it took several minutes to make out. It appeared to me— standing alone in the darkness outside the cabin, looking in through the bedroom window—that Howard was floating naked through space, and it took me the longest time to take the pieces of that optical illusion apart. When I eventually did, it seemed somehow tremendously funny. Howard had painted the room black—floors, walls, ceiling, everything. He had covered his bed with a black blanket. And then, in the manner of Jackson Pollock, he had splashed the room—floors, walls, ceiling, bed, everything—with splotches of luminous

8

white paint. Somewhere in the room he had hidden a black light; and with the darkness outside and the black light shining inside, and with him lying on the bed, he appeared to be floating naked among stars.

The way Howard had decorated his room reminded me of when he was nine or ten years old and a boy scout: when he camped out, he loved to fix up his tent. He liked it better than anything, and he was always stealing things from around our house to use as decorations. I associated that wildly painted room with his old boy scout tents, and it struck me as so amusing that I suddenly felt at ease. I approached the window and knocked at the glass as if I were standing at the front door. "Hey, Buck Rogers!" I called, and this also struck me funny. I bent over and folded my hands across my stomach and laughed so hard my cheeks and jaw and sides started to hurt. When I finally looked up the light was on in the room, and Howard was tying a knot in his black belt. He was flanked by T. J. and McGuinn, and Lieberman was standing on the bed. They were all staring at the window.

I smiled.

Howard opened the window. "Dad," he said, "What are you doing?"

I shrugged and then we smiled at each other. Howard motioned for me to go around to the front of the cabin.

He and T. J. met me on the steps, and I heard McGuinn and Lieberman walking out the back door.

T. J. held out her hand. "I'm very sorry about this afternoon," she said. "I'm really terribly embarrassed."

Her voice was so sweet and her manner and tone so intelligent, that I liked her immensely as soon as I heard her speak a few words. It didn't hurt that she was apologizing—which, at the very least, was an effort at courtesy. I shook her hand. "There's no need to apologize," I said.

"Oh," she said. "I just wish our first meeting had been different." She was barefoot and wearing a pair of baggy jeans and a man's blue cotton work shirt. She clasped her hands together behind her back. "Let's go in," she said, and she stepped back through the door.

Howard started to follow.

"T. J.," I said. "I hope you won't mind, but I'd like to talk to Howard alone for a while. Out here. I'll feel more comfortable out here."

"I understand," she said. "Can I make you some coffee or tea?"

"Coffee," Howard said. "My dad's a big coffee drinker."

T. J. closed the door, and as Howard and I sat alongside each other on the cabin's steps and listened to her, she went about making a pot of coffee.

"She seems like a nice girl," I said.

Howard said, "I love her, Dad. If this were a different time we'd be married."

I shook my head. I didn't want to get into serious matters so quickly. I had hoped we might at least start out talking about the past and sharing memories. I wanted to talk first about those things that joined us before getting to the matters that divided us. But there we were after our first few words and my son was indirectly attacking marriage and the family. I took a deep breath and let it out slowly. "Howard," I said. "I don't understand you, and I really want to. Where can we start?"

Howard shrugged and we were both quiet for a long time. T. J. brought me some coffee, and then we both listened as she went back to her typing. Finally, I asked him what T. J. was writing. She was working on a novel, he told me. That got us started talking, and once we were started we talked through the night while T. J.'s typewriter clattered behind us. Howard believed, he truly believed, that he could love everybody, that we are all beautiful, God-like creatures—and I couldn't make him see it wasn't true. I tried to tell him what poor, desperate animals we all are at heart, but he didn't know what I was talking about, and after awhile I began to feel deranged and unhealthy for trying to make him see things as I saw them.

At dawn T. J. joined us and we walked around to the back of the cabin and watched the sunrise over the ring of mountains. It came up bright and red and it turned a thin line of clouds red all along the horizon. I could almost see Ellie at the motel stumbling out of the bed and shuffling groggily toward the bathroom. Ellie has gotten up at dawn every morning for as long as I've known her. I said, "I've got to go now."

"You're thinking of Mom, aren't you?" Howard said. "She's getting up now."

I laughed and Howard added, "I wish she were here so I could tell her I love her."

The sun had risen clear of the mountains. It was a big, red circle floating above us and casting a red glow over the trees. "I love her too," I said. And we all three sat there quietly a little while longer before I shook Howard's hand and T. J. hugged me, and finally I left. On my way to the trail I passed McGuinn and Lieberman sitting on the front steps. McGuinn was wearing a bright green vest and he had dressed Lieberman in a blue flannel shirt, putting the Chow's legs through the sleeves and buttoning it under his belly. Around the dog's neck he had tied a red bandanna. I waved and McGuinn waved back, but Lieberman just stared intensely. He's never been a very trusting dog.

I've dreamt of that sunrise a number of times since Howard's death, and I must have been dreaming of it again the night of the fire. I awoke to the high-pitched, piercing sound of the smoke alarm, and I don't remember dreaming of anything, but I was groggy and a little dizzy and the living room was filled with a thin haze of smoke and an eerie red glow. For a second before I realized what was happening I thought I heard Howard's voice. I thought I was back at the cabin watching the sunrise. Then I came to my senses. It was a cold night, but the living room was so hot, sweat poured off my body. Ellie was more unconscious than she was asleep, and I had to pick her up and carry her out on my shoulder. When I opened the front door and stepped out into the cold night air, the house seemed to explode behind me. Within minutes there were flames hurrying behind every window, and several hours later the house had burned to rubble—and I watched it burn with Ellie, at first shivering in the cold, and then warm behind a neighbor's window. And all I could think of was Howard. Watching the house where we raised him burn down was like watching his cremation.

He had gotten sick in 1973 and died early in 1974. During those last days in the hospital, he had grown so frail and emaciated that it was hard to look at him. He was twenty-six and he looked like a little old man, his skin sunken around his skeleton, his eyes looking like they might pop out of his head. It took all the courage I had to sit beside him and talk in a normal tone. Ellie couldn't do it. She tried, but toward the end she couldn't look at him without burying her face in her hands and crying, and so she sat in the lounge and waited, trying to build up her strength.

The night before he died, Howard said something to me that I thought I understood but didn't really until the night of the fire. It was late. I had stayed past visiting hours because Howard seemed more alert than usual. He was able to understand what I was saying, and if I bent down and put my ear near to his mouth, I was able to understand his occasional whispered replies. I was trying to tell him, amidst the sickening hospital smells and the fluids dripping through tubes all around us, that his life was the greatest gift Ellie and I had ever been given. But each time I tried to speak I didn't get very far before all my emotions rose up and choked off my voice. Finally I said, "Howard . . . your life . . . your life is like a gift . . ." and I couldn't go on.

Howard motioned with one finger for me to come closer, and he whispered in my ear, "Death is a gift too." When I backed away and looked down at him he said, loud enough for me to hear, "From me to you," and he managed a weak smile.

I thought I knew what he meant then. I thought he meant death would be an end to his suffering, and to my having to watch him suffer. But now I don't think that's what he meant at all. The night of the fire, watching thick flames consume our home, seeing everything I owned drifting away as smoke, I was struck with a physical beauty so solid I could feel it. Death came to me suddenly as a fact, because I saw everything turning in time to dust and ashes—me and Ellie and our house . . . and Howard. I looked at the flames and felt all through me the uniqueness and the beauty of things in time— and often now I feel sure that's what Howard was talking about when he said death was a gift too. It was a revelation when I thought my time of revelations was long gone.

Ellie called from the kitchen. "Joseph, get up!" she yelled. "You've got to see this."

I sat up in bed and looked out the window. The storm clouds were so thick it looked like night out there, but I knew it was midmorning. Still, I didn't feel like getting out of bed. Alongside my pillow, on the mahogany night table, was a copy of T. J.'s first novel. It had just been published by a small press and it wasn't getting much attention, but she was excited about its publication. I hadn't read it yet: it had come in the mail with a long letter the day after the fire. I remember meeting the postman on the street and how we both laughed as he delivered the mail to an acre plot of debris. T. J. said the book wasn't getting many reviews, but the reviews it was getting were good. McGuinn, she told me, had gone back to being a lawyer. He made lots of money these days and dressed very conservatively. She said I wouldn't believe it to see him, but I did. It was 1980 and the country was back to normal. It was like the sixties and seventies had never happened. I hoped McGuinn was happy.

"Joseph!" Ellie called, "Come out here! You're going to miss this!"

I grumbled to myself. I still didn't feel like getting up, but I struggled out of the warm bed and put on my robe and walked out to the kitchen.

For a moment I was disoriented: sunlight poured into the cabin through the bay window and the front door. It was an exceptionally bright day. Then a violent gust of wind slammed the front door closed, and I turned and looked out the back window and the back door, and it was dark as night.

"Wow," I said. I had never seen anything like this and neither had Ellie. Even Lieberman, who had quietly watched our house burn from the distant seclusion of his doghouse and who seemed to want nothing more out of life than to lie somewhere and grow old in silence—even Lieberman was trotting back and forth between the front and back of the cabin and sniffing wildly at the doors.

"Isn't it magnificent!" Ellie said. "Isn't it glorious!"

I nodded. Through the back window I could see the darkness of the storm, and through the front window I could see the mountains rising up around us in bright sunlight. I could see the sky clear and blue beyond the mountains' ridge and I could see the crisp play of light and shadow between the hollows and rises.

"Yes," I answered. "Yes it is."

PRODIGIES

Terry put his hands in his pockets and walked slowly along the concrete sidewalk, a line of cars to his left parked at the curb, his older brother Jay to his right. He was on his way home from the bus stop after his weekly appointment with the school psychiatrist. Terry knew many of the families in this neighborhood: they were mostly Italian and Roman Catholic, and the kids all went to St. Mary's on Sundays.

Jay said, "I think he's nuttier than you are," and stuck his hands into his pockets. Jay was six-one and weighed two hundred and thirty pounds. Before graduating last year, he had played center for his high school football team. He brooded as he trudged along, hunched over and sullen, his size accentuated by his brother's smallness. Terry was five-eight and skinny. He played chess.

Terry took his hands out of his pockets, annoyed by Jay's habit of imitating his stances and gestures.

15

Jay said, "Why do you have to be like this? You got everything going, but no . . . you get an ulcer, you're moody. It's not right for somebody's fourteen. Fourteen and you go to a shrink." He shook his head.

"What do you want from me?"

"Straighten up!"

Terry looked across the street, away from his brother. He wouldn't be going to the shrink at all if his family—his mother and Jay—hadn't insisted. They incorporated it into the family rules, a written document that had been growing in length since the death of his father two years ago. Now it was almost two pages long, single-spaced, every line a rule.

"You going to talk or what?" Jay asked. "How come you never talk to me anymore?"

"I talk to you."

"So? What happened with the shrink? He really tell you this atheism thing's okay?" He spit into the gutter. "He's nuttier than you are."

"You already said that."

"I mean it."

They were still several blocks from home, and Terry was tired of answering questions. The shrink had been pressuring him for an hour. Why this and why that. Why do you feel dead inside? What do you mean, your body feels like it's made out of lead? Why's everything look dark to you? What's your problem, Terry? What's with you? Terry knew the shrink was trying to get him mad, and it had almost worked. When he realized what was up, he just frowned.

Jay caught him by the shoulder. "Just tell me this: Did he say to you 'This atheism thing, it's okay.'?"

"You want to know what he said, Jay?" He started walking again and Jay followed, listening. "I said, 'I don't believe in God.' He said, 'Is it because your father died?' I said, 'I don't think that has much to do with it.' He nodded. I shrugged. That's it. That's all that happened."

"So, then, he didn't say it's okay."

Terry closed his eyes.

Jay thought awhile, and then added, "Well, I take it back. Maybe he's not so nutty."

When they passed Vinnie's house, Vinnie's father and

mother were sitting on the stoop. The father pointed at Terry and spoke to Jay. "You take care of your little brother," he said, wagging his finger. "He'll be a big man one day!"

Jay smiled. "I'll take care of him." He put his hand on Terry's shoulder.

When they were down the block, Terry said, "He always does that. He always tells somebody else how I'm going to be a big man, and I'm standing right there. Why doesn't he ever tell me?"

"'Cause he's shy of you."

"Shit."

"Don't talk like that."

"Why's he shy?"

"Why's he shy. Because he knows you're hot stuff. You're city chess champion—"

"In the fourteen-and-under class."

"You got your picture in the—"

"All right!" Terry said. "That doesn't mean I'm a freak."

Jay stopped. "Who said that? Somebody call you that?"

Terry kept walking.

Jay caught up and held him by the shoulder. "Why you have to be like this?"

Terry didn't answer.

When they reached their block, Jay said: "Will you try to cheer up before we get home, and make Mom feel better."

"I'll cheer up."

"And don't tell her the atheist stuff."

"The shrink said I'm supposed to open up to you and Mom. I'm supposed to tell you what I feel."

"Fine. But not this atheist crap. Mom'll tear her hair out."

"Okay. I won't tell her."

"Anything else, fine. Just not this no God stuff."

"Anything else?"

"Anything. Really."

"Should I tell her I been seeing a girl?"

"What girl? You didn't tell me you been seeing a girl."

"I've been walking her home from the park in the afternoons and hanging out at her house."

"Just the two of you?"

"Her father's home."

"What's her father doing home? Don't he work?"

"He's a teacher. He doesn't work summers."

"Where's he teach?"

"My school."

"You know him?"

"Sure. That's how I met his daughter."

"Who is he? What's he teach?"

Terry was silent for a moment. Then he said, "He's my chess coach."

"The *mulegnane!*" Jay shouted.

Terry turned and stuck his finger in his brother's chest. "Mr. Morris is black," he said, "and I like Johnene a lot, his daughter."

"Okay, okay," Jay said. "I'm sorry I called him a *mulegnane*. But you can't be going out with no black girl. Forget it. Mom'd faint."

"How do you know?" They were in front of their apartment, and Terry sat down on the stoop. Jay sat beside him. The first sporadic clacking and popping of firecrackers began as the sun neared the rooftops.

"They can't wait," Terry said. "Two days before the Fourth, and it sounds like the Fourth already."

From behind him, Roseanna, their mother, threw open the screen on the living room window, which was even with the top of the stoop. She was small and thin and had short hair that made her look pixieish. "I thought I heard you guys."

Jay brushed a caterpillar off his pants. "You got dinner ready yet?"

"Be ready in a minute, King Tut." She closed the screen and disappeared into the apartment.

Jay said, "Let's go up on the roof."

"You tell Mom. I have to go to the bathroom."

Jay led the way into the apartment, and Terry walked quickly through the darkened living room, without looking at the mantel where his mother kept his biggest chess trophies arranged neatly around an enlarged, laminated picture of him with the mayor. The picture was taken after he won the city championship for his age group. The trophies didn't mean anything to Terry, but the checks that came with them meant a lot. The prize money for the city championship was twenty five hundred dollars, which was enough to get the transmission fixed in the car and pay off a third of the VISA bills. Upstairs, in his bedroom, next to his chess computer, he had a pad with all the family's bills listed on one page, and on another page, all the money tournaments held within commuting distance of Brooklyn. So far this year, he had won four thousand dollars, and by the time the year was over he could win another four thousand. That would cut his family's bills in half, and by the end of next year he could have them out of debt; that is, if he kept playing and winning, which he was sure he could do for the next couple of years before he turned sixteen and the competition got tougher. Right now, as far as anybody knew, in his age group he was the best chess player in the city.

When he finished in the bathroom, he joined his mother and brother in the kitchen. Jay was standing by the stove, watching his mother bread the veal cutlets.

Roseanna looked up from her work and leaned over to kiss Terry on the forehead. "How'd it go?"

"Fine."

"Is that all? Fine?"

Jay said, "We're going up on the roof for a little bit, Ma. We'll be right back."

Roseanna tossed a cutlet onto a plate with a bright yellow flower pattern. "Are you guys arguing?"

Jay started for the door.

Terry said, "We're not fighting. We just got some stuff to talk about." He followed Jay, and before he closed the door, he looked back and saw his mother looking after him.

The stairway was dark and windowless. First they passed the door to their bedrooms; then they walked a long hallway which led to a flight of stairs, which led, in turn, to the roof. Terry had two recurring dreams that involved this last flight of stairs. In one, he wanted to get to the top of the steps but couldn't because he could only move two squares diagonally and one horizontally, the way the knight moves in chess. In the dream this made sense. In the other dream, he wanted to get to the top of the stairs again. This time he was at the foot of the stairs, with one hand on the banister. At the top, the door to the roof was just slightly open. There was a bright light behind the door, and a white sliver came through the crack and extended in a thin, straight line that seemed to divide the square landing into equal parts. A gentle tinkling came from behind the door, like wind chimes in a breeze. It sounded to Terry like the most wonderful music. But in this dream, too, Terry was stuck at the bottom of the stairs. His body was too heavy to move, and no matter how hard he tried, forcing and straining, he couldn't climb that last flight leading to the roof. He struggled but couldn't climb even a single step. In some of the dreams, he'd hear something behind him in the dark, and he'd try to flip on a light switch as whatever it was behind him moved closer, but the switch would flip up and down, and the light wouldn't come on. In those dreams, he wanted to climb the stairs so badly that even when he remembered the dream wide awake, he felt a kind of pang inside, a sadness that made him feel empty, as if his life were a blank, a zero. As if nothing worthwhile were ever going to happen to him.

"There he is," Jay said as they stepped onto the tarpaper roof. He was referring to Pigeon, the house painter who lived in the apartment below them, and spent most of his spare time on the roof, usually caring for his flock of pigeons, which he kept in a wire coop. Pigeon's real name was William, and Terry liked him. He liked to see the flock being turned loose, the way they roared out of their cage like a blast of wind; and he liked the way Pigeon called to them and talked to them, with a gesture of his arm sending the signals to move them one way or another. For a while, when Terry was thirteen, he had come up here often, usually evenings after school, to share a joint with Pigeon and listen to him talk about Jesus Christ, which was Pigeon's favorite subject. He believed Christ was coming back to save the world, and he believed it would happen soon. "Within my lifetime," he'd say, and point to the sky. "He's coming!"

Pigeon's view of Christianity, though, was odd. He didn't believe in sin and he didn't believe in hell. "Forget all that Sunday School stuff," he'd say. "Forget about what you should do and what you shouldn't, and who's right and who's wrong. Christ is love! Christ is the light!" When he got really excited, he'd raise his hands to the sky, and his ten fingers would waver like the flickering flames of votive candles.

Jay didn't like Pigeon. Last year he had caught them sharing a joint, and Pigeon had had to run downstairs and lock himself in his apartment and barricade the door to keep Jay from tearing his arms off—which is what Jay had been yelling: "I'm tearing your arms off, you freak! I'll tear off your arms!" Eventually it all got straightened out when Terry promised never to smoke grass again and not to hang out with Pigeon. On those conditions—which became part of the family rules—Jay had allowed Pigeon's arms to remain in place. But he still didn't like him.

"Hey, Pigeon," Jay said. "Would you mind letting me and Terry have the roof for a few minutes. We have to talk."

Pigeon nodded, threw a handful of feed into the coop, and started for the door. He was wearing a white T-shirt with a picture of Jesus Christ on the front, Christ's expanded heart rising out of his chest in flames, giving off streams of yellow light that flew outward and looked as though they might leap off the shirt. At the door, Pigeon said, "I'm done for now anyway," and then disappeared down the stairs.

Jay shook his head.

"He's okay," Terry said. "I miss watching him fly the pigeons and listening to his crazy talk, if you want to know the truth." He sat on the narrow roof cresting.

"Don't sit there," Jay said.

Terry slid down and sat on the tarpaper roof.

Jay sat beside him. "You can't be dating no black girl. It'd kill Mom, and the whole family'd be nuts."

"Don't tell me that." Terry closed his eyes. "I can't believe you're going to be like this."

"It's not me," Jay said. "I got nothing against them. It's Mom. You're going to bring home a black girl? She'd go through the floor. You can't do it. Plus, you know how the rest of the family feels about blacks. They'd spit on you. The whole neighborhood."

"What about me?" Terry said. He stared at the pigeon coop.

"Well," Jay started to get up. "I'm sorry. Honest, Terry. But you shouldn't have started fooling around with a black girl. You should have known better."

Terry said, "What about if I bring her over to meet Mom?"

"No."

"Why?"

"'Cause it's not going to change anything. She'll still be black."

Terry was shaking a little bit and he felt his stomach knotting up, but he got to his feet nonchalantly. "Well, I'm not listening to you. I don't care what you say."

"Do I have to bring up Dad again? Do I always have to do that?"

"Leave my father out of this."

Jay's face turned red. "*Your* father? What? He wasn't my father too? Is that what you're saying?"

"Your father lives on Ainslie Street."

"You little bastard." Jay picked him up by the collar and pinned him against the pigeon coop. "Nobody's seen that son of a bitch since I was a baby. He don't mean nothing to anybody and you're just bringing him up because you're mad at me."

"He's still your father."

Jay tightened his grip and pushed harder. "You're going to do like I tell you," he said. "Just like you promised Dad." He backed up and let Terry go. Then he walked to the stairs with his hands in his pockets and nudged the door open with his shoulder. He went down without bothering to close the door behind him.

When the sound of his brother's footsteps faded away, Terry went to the edge of the roof and looked over. His knees felt watery. It was getting late, and firecrackers were going off all around the neighborhood. The huge blasts of cherry bombs and ash cans and M16s punctuated the machine-gun rattle of exploding packs of firecrackers. Occasionally the sky would light up with the colored flares of Roman candles. Terry told himself it didn't matter that he couldn't see Johnene. Nothing mattered. "What do I care," he said aloud, and he breathed deeply, his bottom lip trembling a little.

22

The streetlights had come on a while ago, and now lights were on in all the apartments. Up and down the block, people were coming out to their stoops, escaping the heat of their homes. Terry watched the people and the lights, and he listened to the fireworks and watched for the bright flashes and flares. It felt strangely like watching a movie. He hardly seemed to be there at all. The people moved around as if they were on a screen, and he felt as though he were in a theatre where the air was thick as water. On the corner, someone walked out from under the light of a street lamp and into a shadow, and the movement reminded Terry of a chess piece moving from a white to a black square. When he squinted, he could make all the pockets of light and shadow throughout the neighborhood become squares on a huge chessboard. He imagined all the movement he saw as if it were in accordance with the game's rules; and thinking about chess made him feel comfortable, as it always had, ever since he played his first game with his father when he was five years old.

When Terry played chess, time stopped and the world disappeared. There was nothing but the game. Often he wished that his father could come back for just one night, so he could show him how good he had become. His father was himself an expert chess player who had won several city tournaments. Terry had never won a game against him. It was in the year after his father's death that his talents really developed. Sick, in the hospital, only a few weeks away from dying, Terry's father had sent everyone out of the room and motioned Terry to sit on the bed alongside him.

"What's going on?" Terry asked.

His father said, "I have something for you," and he took a box wrapped in aluminum foil out from under the sheets.

Terry unwrapped the package and found the chess computer. At the time, it was the best computer on the market. He cried when he opened it, because he knew that his father had given it to him to replace him as a chess partner when he was gone. His father had held him in his arms for a long time then, until a nurse interrupted them. After his father died, Terry played the computer every chance he got. Now it never beat him any more. Never.

Below him, on the street, there was a loud crash and the sound of glass breaking. He looked down and saw a kid his own age running away from a shattered milk bottle.

Then he heard his mother's voice. She spoke softly and he could tell she was standing behind him in the open doorway. "Your dinner's like ice."

He hesitated a second before acknowledging her. The noise from the city below him kept growing—firecrackers, people, cars, distant sirens—but it all seemed oddly one-dimensional, movie-like. The loud noise felt like a great quiet, and the light seemed dull and unmoving, like the light in an old picture or a painting.

"I'm coming," he said, and he joined his mother by the door, putting his arm around her waist. He leaned against her and they walked down the stairs.

*　　*

Johnene's father was a funny looking man. His body parts seemed all out of proportion. He had spindly legs that disappeared into a pot belly. His arms were fat, his neck thin, and his head oversized. The man was constantly in motion, usually laughing. Just looking at him made Terry giggle. At the moment, he was laughing in anticipation of the ending of a story he was telling Terry. Terry grinned like a moron, waiting to hear what was so funny. This was dangerous because often what Mr. Morris found funny was a pure mystery to everyone else. But Terry was listening intently, as usual, and waiting for the punch line.

Mr. Morris was standing in front of a sink full of soapy water, about to wash the dishes, and Terry was sitting at the kitchen table, which he had just helped clear. Johnene had run upstairs for a minute. When he finally quit laughing, Mr. Morris ended his story, waving a spoon at Terry as if he were conducting an orchestra, droplets of thick, red spaghetti sauce flying up onto the ceiling. Terry laughed, though once again he wasn't sure what was so funny.

Johnene came hurrying down the stairs and into the kitchen carrying a boxed chess set under her arm. She was a tiny, wiry girl, with short hair cropped close to her head. "Come on," she said to Terry. She was wearing jeans and a bright red blouse.

Mr. Morris said, "Where you going? Terry and I were in the middle of a conversation, weren't we Terry?"

Terry nodded. "Your dad was just telling me a story."

This threw Mr. Morris into a new fit of laughter.

Johnene frowned. "Are you teaching me?" She held up the chess set.

Terry got up and slid his chair back under the table.

Johnene said to her father, "We're going out to the courtyard."

"The courtyard?" Mr. Morris grinned. "You're going out to the courtyard to play chess, uh huh. You think I'm senile, girl?"

"Dad," Johnene said. "Don't embarrass me."

Mr. Morris put on a straight face. "I'm sorry dear." He turned to Terry, his hand over his mouth, straining to sound serious. He couldn't, however, keep from laughing. He said, "You just watch how much you teach her, son!"

When Terry and Johnene left the kitchen, Mr. Morris was laughing so hard he had to hold the sink for support.

"That man's crazy," Johnene said as they stepped out into the courtyard. The courtyard was a tiny roofless space enclosed by brick walls. Actually, it was shaped more like an alley than a courtyard. When Johnene and her father first moved into the apartment, the space was piled high with years of junk. But Johnene had liked the texture of the red brick walls, and with her father's help she had cleaned up the junk, scrubbed the inner walls and floor, and put in benches and a small table, and rows of plants along the walls. Together they had turned the space into a courtyard. Now it was Johnene's favorite place.

Terry set up the chess pieces on the table. "I don't think he's crazy," he said. "I think he's great."

Johnene was sitting on the bench against the wall, watching Terry. "He likes you too," she said. "He thinks you're great."

"Maybe I'll get him for English next year."

"That'd be cool."

Terry finished setting up the pieces. He turned to Johnene and caught her looking solemnly at the ground. "What's wrong?"

She didn't answer.

He sat alongside her. "What is it?"

"My mother." She made a face. "I talked to her last night. She's moved in with her new boyfriend."

Terry said, "You knew she was going to, didn't you?"

"I don't know why I let it bother me."

Terry saw that her eyes were watery, and he touched her hand. Her skin felt soft and warm, and as soon as he touched her, his heart speeded up and his throat tightened.

Johnene leaned close to him and he put his arm around her. Together they leaned back against the brick wall. First Terry kissed her lightly on the forehead, and then Johnene leaned away from him and said, "I thought you were *never* going to get around to kissing me." Terry felt feathery all over. He felt so light, he thought he might float away. He moved closer to Johnene and touched his lips to hers, and then they were pressing into each other, their tongues meeting and touching, their hands grasping each other's bodies, squeezing and holding as if they were trying to pull themselves into each other. This kept up until the light started to fade above them, and Terry's legs and back and arms were sore from so much hard wrestling. He felt sure Johnene must feel the same way. When he finally pulled himself away from her, he touched his fingers to his lips, half expecting to find them blistered.

They were sitting on the floor now, having gone through every possible position on the bench. Their clothing was disheveled, and every button and zipper between the two of them was unsnapped and undone. Terry said, "Wow, Johnene. I really think you're great."

Johnene pointed at the darkening sky. For the past hour, fireworks had been going off all over the city, and now it was beginning to sound like a war was going on outside the little courtyard. "Don't you have to be home before dark? Isn't that one of your 'family rules'?"

Terry nodded.

"Won't your brother be mad?"

He thought for a moment, and then said, "He'll just have to understand." He put his arm around Johnene. Overhead, a flickering street lamp came on, filling the courtyard with a bouncy, wavering light. Terry and Johnene moved back into a corner, and Terry watched the light in the courtyard while he held Johnene close to his chest. The light seemed to be moving like water, rippling and flowing all around them. He said to Johnene, "Look at the way the light moves like water," and Johnene said, "It looks like a river," and rearranged herself in his arms so that her cheek was touching the bare skin of his neck, and at that touch something moved inside Terry. It felt as though something within him had turned over in its sleep.

Johnene said, "Look at the chess set."

Terry looked at the board and pieces where they sat on the table in the center of the courtyard, the lamp light washing away the crisp lines of the squares. "What about it?" he asked.

"Look at the way the light makes the pieces move."

It was dark out now, and the air was full of whistling and explosions, and every few minutes the sky above the courtyard lit up with brightly colored flares. Terry looked hard at the chess set until he saw how the light came down like rain and made the pieces on the chessboard dance. Inside him, whatever it was that had moved before, moved again.

THE
FOALING
MAN

Nicholas patted the star on Molly's forehead, rubbed his cheek against her nose, and said, "You're looking serious tonight, Molly. Is it time to foal?"

Molly pushed her forehead against his chest and moved her head vigorously up and down.

"Yes, yes," he said, and when she had finished using his chest as a scratching board he patted her gently on the neck and left her stall.

In the aisle of the foaling shed he sat down on the hard-packed dirt. At twenty-three he still looked like a teenager. His face remained pale in spite of outdoor work, and he carried into his twenties a look of innocence. His arms and chest and legs, however, were heavily muscled. He rested his back against the wooden half-door of Molly's stall, brought his legs to his chest, and propped his chin on his knees. Outside, a storm was building. A long line of black clouds was crossing the Shawangunk Mountains and moving east across the Hudson Valley. He watched their progress as they moved slowly toward him trailing darkness.

A gust of wind blew through the shed scattering straw and dust, and Nicholas covered his eyes with his forearm. Above him, Molly lowered her head over the stall door and rubbed her nose against the back of his neck. He reached up and scratched her cheek, and she bit him on the collar, playfully, but hard enough to hurt. He slapped her on the nose and she whinnied and jumped back into the stall.

From the other end of the aisle, where the shed made a right angle turn to form a short L-shaped structure which accommodated one extra stall and a breeding area, Nicholas heard Hawk scream. Hawk was the Blue R breeding farm's stud. All the mares in this shed were carrying his foals.

"You hear that, Molly?" he said. "Hawk's calling you. He's concerned."

Behind him Molly was standing motionless, staring with an otherworldly look at the wooden planks of her stall.

On the whole farm, Hawk was the only horse Nicholas didn't like. He found the stud's temperament maddening. It was not just that the horse was dangerous, but that it was arrogant and disdainful. Being the most valuable horse on the farm, Hawk had been treated specially for so long that he had come to believe he was special. He acted as though he were the center of the universe, and he demanded that his handlers treat him as such. Nicholas wanted to beat Hawk senseless, to pound him until his knees buckled and that look of disdain was replaced by pleading—like a dog fearing a kick from his master.

"Hey Molly?" he said. "Molly?" Then he laughed at himself because he half expected her to answer, to at least whinny or stamp her foot in the straw.

Back in Brooklyn Nicholas had frightened his family by not speaking until he was almost three years old, and all through his youth—and, for that matter, into his present adulthood—he had a hard time speaking to others. But here on the farm, working the night watch alone from six at night to six in the morning, he felt at ease and found he liked talking to horses. At first he was embarrassed and felt as if he were acting a little crazy, but he soon learned that everyone talked to horses, perhaps not as much as he did at times, especially late at night when a kind of fear sometimes took hold, but it was something everyone did. Even old Albie, the farm manager, cursed them, calling them "nickel bastards"; and Doc Will talked to the horses as he worked on them. Will could calm a horse enough with his talking to slip a worming hose down its nose and into its stomach without a fuss. He lived nearby and was considered by many the best veterinarian in the state, some said the country. If he could talk to horses, so could Nicholas. Besides, Nicholas half believed they understood what he said, especially Molly.

When he first came to the Blue R he was twenty-one and didn't know anything about horses. That was two years ago; now he felt like an old hand. There wasn't a horse on the farm he was afraid of, including Hawk, and because of that he had earned the respect of Albie and the other farm hands who had come and gone since he was hired. The Blue R underpaid all its workers, so most of them only stuck around long enough to save up traveling money. But Albie and Nicholas stayed on: Albie, because he was too old to find a decent job anywhere else, and Nicholas, because he had nowhere else to go. He had lived in Brooklyn all his life until he walked out of the city, with only twenty dollars in his wallet and no idea where he was going. He wound up a couple of days later at the Blue R.

Nicholas associated everything bad in his life with Brooklyn. It was in Brooklyn that his younger sister had disappeared one day while shopping with him and his mother in a five-and-dime. One moment she was there and then she was gone. Fifteen years later Nicholas still sometimes replayed the incident. He had left her alone in the toy aisle to go after his mother and when he returned she was gone. She turned up several weeks later floating in the East River, her hands and feet hacked off. A few years later his mother died of cancer. It was diagnosed in April and she was dead in June. He lived with his father until he graduated from high school, and then he left home for an apartment of his own and a factory job in a plant on Manhattan Avenue. For the next two years he lived alone—until he decided one day to walk past his bus stop and to keep walking, first over the Kosciusko Bridge, then hitch-hiking, taking rides without direction, going wherever his ride was going.

He still considered it his wisest decision—if it could be called a decision, spontaneous as it was. He had come to love horses and he liked working at the Blue R, especially as the foaling man. When he first saw the farm it stirred something in him: something seemed to loosen up and then expand at the sight of acres of green pasture filled with horses. He had found the Blue R by asking around Wallkill—where a truck driver had let him off—for a job, and once given directions he walked the six miles from town. Molly was the first horse to notice him as he walked down the hill at the entrance to the farm. There was a bird lighted on her shoulder, chirping, and two or three more on the ground around her head, eating grain in the grass where she was grazing. She picked up her head at the sight of him and whinnied and then trotted along the fence line alongside him till he walked past. Nicholas stopped and looked at her before continuing down the hill to a place where he saw a white truck parked in bright sunlight outside the dark entrance to the main barn. As he approached, he heard the voices of men yelling to each other, and then three men came running out of the darkness and scattered when they hit the sunlight. Hawk came prancing out after them, screaming.

He was a big, muscular horse, and black from head to foot, so black his coat seemed to soak up the sun. Nicholas watched, enthralled, as Hawk screamed and reared, pummeling the air with his forelegs. At first he felt exhilarated watching the stal-lion, but when Hawk saw him and looked at him as if he were deciding whether to kill such a puny thing, Nicholas felt some-thing harden within him. He walked calmly to the horse. Hawk, to the amazement of the farmhands watching from a dis-tance, took several steps backward, apparently stunned by a man walking toward him instead of running away. Nicholas took the stud by the lead shank dangling from his halter and waited until a farm hand came and led Hawk away.

That was how he got his job at the Blue R. He started muck-ing out stalls, and then loading hay, and finally he got to handle horses. Now he was the foaling man. It was his job to come in every night, water first Hawk and then each of the twenty-four mares in foal, examine all the mares, and assist any that foaled. This last part of his job was what Nicholas most enjoyed.

Since mares are private about foaling, he had to play a careful game of hide-and-seek. He would keep himself well out of sight until the irreversible process began, and then quietly enter the stall and help with the foaling. His job was easy, and for the most part superfluous. The mares did not need him to help pull the foal out of the womb, as he did, nor did they need him to drag the foal around to the mother's head, so she could see it and lick the slime from its nose and mouth. The important part of Nicholas's job was that he be there if something went wrong, and there were many things that could go wrong. A mare, for instance, might reject her foal and try to kill it, or an umbilical cord might fail to clot properly, which could cause a foal to bleed to death in minutes. In a dangerous case, Nicholas would call Doc Will. So far they had not lost a single foal.

Nicholas was proud of this record, and he liked watching the new foals as they struggled to get to their feet in a new world of shapes and colors and sounds. But in all the foals, within a few hours after birth, Nicholas saw hints of their sire's demeanor. Something of the pride and insensitivity of Hawk showed itself through a glimmer in the foal's eyes, or in a stance that it assumed instinctively.

A few months after he had started working at the Blue R, he had his shoulder broken by Hawk. It wasn't the injury that galled him so much as the way it happened. Hawk was standing peacefully in his stall, looking calmly out the barred window at the top of the back wall, when Nicholas entered with the hose and started to refill his water bucket. Hawk backed away from the window—still calmly, peacefully, as if he were paying Nicholas no attention—and when he was within striking distance, he threw a series of kicks with his hind legs. The first one came so close to striking a killing blow that he felt a hoof graze his right ear. Another blow caught him in the shoulder before he could get out of the stall.

Still, he could have forgiven that; but a few days later there was another incident. May Pride was a good-sized mare, but she had foaled a runt. The little colt, aside from looking funny (he had floppy ears and a tail that almost touched the ground), had a problem with his back left pastern—a swelling that sometimes appears in young horses and usually goes away as they put on size and weight. So the colt walked with a funny gait. Nicholas had tied him up in the breeding shed one afternoon while he drove the truck to the back pasture to pick up a tool he had forgotten there. When he returned he found the runt dead and Hawk wandering through the stable. Hawk had gotten out of his paddock and found the runt. What bothered Nicholas most was that the runt, because of the way he was tied with his head in the corner, could not have seen what was happening. For Nicholas, this made everything worse.

Nicholas was thinking about Hawk and the runt, thinking that just once he would like to tie Hawk in a corner and make him grovel, when he heard a grumbling noise. He stood and looked into Molly's stall. She hadn't moved and was still staring intently at the wall. Nicholas guessed it was just her stomach he had heard and he reached in and patted her gently on the shoulder. He was about to say something to her when Hawk screamed, and his scream was echoed by a flash of lightning and a low rumble of thunder.

"Is it water you want, Hawk?" Nicholas shouted. In the distance Hawk whinnied, as if in response. "All right," he said quietly, "I'm coming." He picked up his denim jacket from the ground, put it on, and took his flashlight out from between the bars of Molly's stall.

Outside, the rain began to fall. Nicholas buttoned his jacket and walked to the opposite end of the shed. The thin beam of the flashlight danced in front of him as he followed the shed aisle, and all along the way mares stared at him through the bars of their stalls.

The spigot and hose were located directly across from Hawk's stall. Nicholas paid no attention to the stud standing ominously alongside his water bucket; he stared, instead, through the window in Hawk's stall, at the driving rain falling across the dark fields. A flash of lightning broke the darkness, and in that instant of white-blue light the lifeless fields were lit up, revealing clusters of horses standing asleep in the wind and rain. Hawk pawed at the ground, making a low, guttural, growling noise.

Nicholas turned and looked at the stud. "Tonight, Hawk," he said softly, "you can wait for your water." He unwound the long coil of hose and walked past Hawk's stall. He began the nightly rounds with Lady Be Fast.

Hawk looked confused as Nicholas walked by without stopping to fill his bucket, and when he heard a mare's bucket being filled, he started kicking at the walls and screaming. Inside Lady Be Fast's stall, Nicholas could not keep himself from smiling. Good, he thought. You bastard. Wait for your water.

It took a long time for Hawk to calm down. The stallion stopped kicking just as a long, sizzling flash of lightning struck close by, shaking the rafters of the shed. Nicholas closed a stall door behind him and hesitated for a moment in the shed aisle. When he heard nothing more than Hawk's angry pawing and the rain, he continued with his watering.

With only Molly and Hawk left to water, he stopped for a rest in front of Molly's stall. She had a strange look about her. Her muscles were tensed, as if she were in pain.

"What's the matter, Molly?" Nicholas slid open the door to her stall. "Are you going to foal tonight? Is that your problem?"

Molly stood quietly, staring intently at a thick plank of wood.

He patted her gently on the head; then walked around alongside her, stroking her neck and shoulders. "Is it time, Molly?" he asked. "You look terrible." From the other end of the shed came a loud crash and the sound of metal crumpling. Molly picked up her ears. "Just Hawk kicking his water bucket," Nicholas said. He walked in front of her. "I'm not mean, am I Molly?" He scratched the insides of her ears. "No," he answered. "I'm not mean." He finished his examination and having found nothing wrong patted her once more on the neck. "Now that I'm ready," he said, "I'll go water the bastard."

As he picked up the hose, Hawk began kicking; but by the time he reached the stall, the stallion was motionless, his nose pressed to the crumpled rim of the water bucket. A white froth of sweat stood out against the sleek black of his coat.

"What's the matter, Hawk? Are you upset? Didn't I bring you your water on time?" Nicholas pushed the door open a crack and slipped into the stall.

Hawk remained still, his nose pressed against the battered rim of the pail. Nicholas closed the stall door behind him and pulled a length of hose slowly through the metal bars. He gripped the gun-like nozzle in his left hand, leaving his right hand free, and moved carefully toward Hawk, until he stood alongside him.

Hawk looked as if he were asleep, but Nicholas could see the tension in the long sheets of muscle running down his neck and shoulders and across his back to his legs. Carefully, with his right hand clenched in a fist, he pushed down firmly on the handle. With the first sound of water rushing against the metal of the pail, Hawk jumped up on his back legs, screamed, and struck out at Nicholas with his forelegs.

Nicholas cursed and ducked. He tried, while staying away from the forelegs, to grab the stud's halter, but Hawk slammed him against the wall with his rump. The breath knocked out of him, Nicholas staggered and then lurched for the stall door, but Hawk barred the way by throwing a series of blows with his rear legs. Nicholas tripped and fell into the corner, where he cut his elbow on the ragged rim of the water bucket and hit his head against the metal bars before falling to the ground. Shaking his head, trying to regain his senses—the corners of his vision clouded with a soft, green mosaic—he reached up and grabbed for the bucket. He tried to pull himself to his feet before Hawk could come at him again, but the bucket broke from its hook.

On his back, in the straw, with the bucket alongside him, he looked up to see Hawk standing on his rear legs and moving toward him, shrieking and snorting. As he backed away from the stud and tried to prop himself up against the wall, he felt, in the straw beneath his hand, the cold metal nozzle of the hose. Thrusting it in front of him with both hands, he shot a stream of water into Hawk's flaring nostrils. Hawk almost fell over backward as he jumped away from the water, into the opposite corner of the stall.

Nicholas pulled himself weakly to his feet, aiming the hose at Hawk as if it were a weapon. "You want your water?" he said. "Here . . ." He grabbed the bucket off the ground and flung it across the stall. "There's your goddamned water!"

In the shed aisle, he slammed the stall door closed. .

Hawk snorted and pawed at the ground.

"We're going to come to an understanding," Nicholas whispered to himself. He walked away from Hawk to an unoccupied stall, where he sat down on the dirt floor and wrapped his handkerchief around the cut on his elbow. Outside, beyond the barn wall, he could hear the rain falling hard upon the already water-soaked grass, and as he listened he recalled Hawk jumping away from the water. Thinking about his small victory, he closed his eyes and lay down in the dirt and the darkness. Within a few minutes, with only the sound of the rain and the occasional whinny of a mare in the background, he was sleeping.

When he awoke, the rain had stopped falling and the barn was filled with the first sounds of morning. He lifted himself to his feet, brushed the dirt from his shirt and pants, and walked, yawning and stretching, to Molly's stall.

She was already foaling. Her body slick with sweat, she looked up at him weakly, with a look of resignation: a foal, like a diver in midair, its head tucked between its legs, was protruding halfway out her swollen womb. The water sac was broken, and the foal's coat was wet and slimy. Nicholas watched, at first delighted, as the foal wiggled its head and, blinking a few times, opened its eyes; but when Molly's body heaved in a violent contraction and the foal didn't move any further out of the womb, he realized something was wrong.

He hurried into the stall, clasped his hands around the foal's outstretched legs, and pulled. It didn't budge. He changed positions: propping his feet against Molly's buttocks, he pulled with his whole body. Still, the foal didn't move. It just picked up its head and looked at him, appearing for all the world to be merely curious.

When all the strength was gone from his arms, he ran to the phone and called Doc Will, then returned to the stall. Molly's eyes were milky and glazed, but she still followed Nicholas's movements as he knelt in the straw at her head and spoke softly to her. "The vet's on his way, Molly," he said, rubbing her forehead.

Molly moved slightly and bared her teeth as if she were going to neigh, but made no sound. Nicholas continued talking softly to her and rubbing her forehead, trying to comfort her, until he heard the vet's station wagon pull up in front of the shed.

Will nodded summarily at Nicholas as he walked into the stall, and then stared at Molly and the foal. He was wearing a raincoat, inside out, over a pair of striped pajamas, and carrying a large black leather satchel.

He walked around to the foal, put his bag down alongside its head, and, while the foal watched, took off both his raincoat and the top of his pajamas. From the black bag he pulled out a pair of disposable plastic gloves and slipped them over his hands, all the way up to his shoulders.

Carefully, he slid his hands down the foal's chest and pushed his arm deep into Molly's womb. The foal made a sound near enough to laughter to startle both Nicholas and the vet.

"Jesus," Nicholas said, smiling. "It's laughing. It doesn't know what's going on."

Will didn't respond. Half kneeling and half lying in the straw, with his temple pushed flush against Molly's rectum and his arms buried up to his shoulders, the doctor struggled to maneuver the foal into a deliverable position. He stayed that way—sweating, pushing, pulling, and shoving—for several minutes before extracting his arms and taking off the gloves, an edge of disgust in the way he looked and moved.

He spoke to Nicholas as he wiped Molly's dirt from his forehead and hair. "In the back of my wagon, underneath the spare tire and some other junk, there's a bolt cutter. Go get it."

Nicholas didn't understand. "A bolt cutter?"

Will pulled an assortment of instruments out of his bag and laid them neatly on an unrolled strip of cloth. Nicholas hesitated a moment longer and then left the stall.

Outside, the fields were filled with the first blue haze of morning light, and a thick mist covered the rain-soaked grass. He pulled open the back door of the station wagon and after some rummaging, found the bolt cutter and brought it back into the shed.

It took him a few moments, standing in the doorway of the stall, to understand what he was looking at. The vet had made a long, circular incision around the width of the foal's body. Having pushed back several inches of loose skin, he was pulling out its intestines and tossing them into a corner of the stall. The foal was cut neatly in half. The abdomen and torso remained attached only by the backbone.

Nicholas felt a slow calm settle over him. He walked into the stall and dropped, half threw, the bolt cutter down at the vet's feet.

Will looked up at him as if he were suddenly aware of the presence of a stranger and pointed to a place, high on the foal's back, where a section of spine was exposed. "Take the bolt cutter," he said, "and snap it—right there."

Nicholas picked up the tool and positioned it carefully over the spine. He cut the backbone easily in half. The foal's torso fell limply into the vet's waiting arms. The head hung loosely from the neck, and the tongue spilled out of the mouth.

Will threw the torso out into the shed aisle and sutured the flap of skin hanging over the exposed abdominal cavity. After the cavity was sewn closed he pushed the posterior half of the foal back inside the womb, and with only a few seconds of maneuvering he was able to pull it free. Nicholas watched as the vet held the mutilated carcass dangling in the air, the fur wet and black and spotted with blood.

"A colt," Will muttered, and he tossed the half-foal out of the stall, where it landed, grotesquely, on top of the torso.

Nicholas knelt in the straw at Molly's head and patted her neck gently, as if to comfort her, while the vet put on a new pair of gloves and inserted his arms once again inside her to reexamine the womb. When he was finished he said nothing, but he shook his head slightly as he took a syringe from his bag, filled it with a syrupy white fluid, and injected it into a vein in Molly's neck.

Molly blinked a few times and then closed her eyes.

Nicholas looked up at the doctor. "Did you knock her out?" he asked.

Will spit in the straw. "I put her to sleep," he said. "She was too badly damaged. She would have been dead by morning." Nicholas felt tears in the corners of his eyes.

Will turned away. He took off his gloves and wiped his hands clean on a rag; then he unbuttoned his fly and urinated in a corner of a stall. After he put on his pajama top and raincoat, he started to walk away but stopped in the doorway. "There's nothing anyone could have done," he said. "It was . . . Tell Albie I'll be around again in the evening."

Nicholas wanted to say something, but he felt ashamed and knew he wouldn't be able to speak without sobbing, so he nodded and didn't look up. After the vet's wagon pulled away, he cried.

As morning light spread through the stall, he stood—his knees uncertain beneath him—and walked the length of the shed. When he came to Hawk's stall, he picked up the hose and entered. With Hawk half asleep and paying him no attention, and with the nightmarish screaming of birds all around him, he took the bucket out and hammered the crumpled rim into a reasonable circle. Then, hanging it neatly in its corner, he filled it with water.

SILVER
DOLLARS

———

Alice gave Coon two subway tokens and told him to go ride the trains for a few hours. Coon, angry, snatched the tokens from her hand and started for the door. "Coon," Alice said, "we'll play a game of checkers tonight, after supper." Coon turned in the doorway. They lived in the basement apartment of a three-story house in Brooklyn. It was four o'clock and the late-afternoon sun came in through the window at Coon's shoulder, a window dressed with bare, white Venetian blinds, and it fell in strips across the room. Coon looked as though he were standing behind bars. "You promise?" he asked. He looked a little worried. "A whole game?"

"After supper," Alice said, "I promise."

Coon hesitated in the doorway. Alice was sixteen, five years older than Coon, but he felt that she needed him to look after her. She was stupid about people. Once last year one of the college guys she was always picking up got her pregnant. When she told Coon, she put her head in his lap and cried. At first he was angry and he pulled away from her. Then he paced around the room looking, at ten years old, exactly like a little man, like a miniature father. "Why'd you let him get you pregnant?" he asked. "How could you?"

Alice wiped the tears away. "What do you know about it?"

"More than you, it looks like."

Tears welled up in Alice's eyes again. "He said he was using something!" she shouted. "How was I supposed to know? He said!"

Coon shook his head. "How were you supposed to know," he repeated.

Later he stole some money to help her get it taken care of. Coon was a good thief. He could find a way into most any apartment in Brooklyn when he wanted to, most any apartment in the city, he guessed. But before he gave her the money he made her promise one thing: "You never call me your pet brother again. You never call me that to anybody."

Alice looked sad when he said that. "Where'd you hear me call you that, Coon?" she asked, but before he could answer she said, "I'm sorry, Coon. I'm real sorry," and she held him in her arms and cried.

For a while they just sat there in the dimly lit living room of their parents' apartment, alone, with Alice crying. Coon had a dark purple birthmark that came down from his temples in a band that covered his eyes like a mask, which is why he was called Coon. It was because of that birthmark, he thought, that no one in the world ever treated him right. "You just never call me that again," Coon said, and Alice nodded and hugged him tighter. Since then Coon had never heard her call him her pet brother, but she still called him Coon. Everyone did, even though, except for the birthmark, he was a strikingly handsome kid: a thin, small boy with straight, dusty-brown hair that made an attractive contrast with his skin, which was very light—not pale, but delicate-looking, fragile-looking skin. In the summer he had to be careful to stay out of the sun, because he burned so easily, and in the winter it seemed he could never get warm enough. His facial features, also, were delicate, almost feminine: he was a pretty child, or at least he would have been a pretty child, if not for the birthmark.

Coon stepped back into the apartment. "You've got one of those jerks from college coming over again, don't you?"

Alice said, "Stop acting like you're my father!" and she put all her weight on one leg and her hands on her hips, and she rocked in a way Coon couldn't bear to look at.

He left, slamming the door behind him. Once outside he opened the window, stuck his arm through the blinds, and tossed the two tokens Alice had given him into the kitchen at her feet.

Alice turned away from the mirror that hung alongside the kitchen stove, where she had been fixing her hair. "I forgot," she said. "My little brother's a hot shot. He doesn't need tokens to ride the trains."

Coon made a face. "Don't forget to get him out of here by six-thirty and get supper going for Mom and Dad."

"I know, I know," Alice said.

He added, "And you still look like a jerk." Then he slammed the window and started down the block.

One day last week Alice had shown up for supper with her hair cut short, slicked back on one side, and dyed orange and platinum. "It's punk," she said. "It's the latest." Their father's face turned about the same colors as Alice's hair, but for all his screaming and slamming things around, and threatening, Alice wouldn't budge. It was the style, and she liked it. Finally he cursed her and his whole family and went out to get drunk, which was something he did a couple of times a month anyway. Later that night, their mother tried to talk to her, but when Alice told her to mind her own business and leave her alone, she quietly retreated to the living room where she took a seat in front of the TV and turned on one of her shows. So, for a week now Alice had looked this way. She had always worn tight-fitting clothes that showed off her body, but now the skirts were even shorter and tighter, and she had stopped wearing a bra and started wearing flimsy, ragged shirts, so that, as far as Coon could see, she might as well be naked from the waist up. It bothered Coon. He wanted her to be ladylike, but instead she was . . . Her word was the best. She was punk.

Coon stepped onto a subway train heading for uptown Manhattan. He took a seat and watched the graffiti-covered doors slide closed. In a minute the train lurched and then was off rattling and rocking through the long, dark tunnels. He sat back in the harsh yellow light of the car and looked at his reflection in the window across from him. He stared at his eyes peering back from behind their black mask. When he grew up, he thought, he wanted to be a big-time thief, maybe a murderer. He wanted people to be scared of him and do whatever he told them. "If I say jump," he said aloud to his reflection, "they'd better jump!" He was alone in his car—all the traffic this time of day was going the other way—and he felt comfortable among the familiar shrieks and howls of the subway. He laid his head back against the glass and looked up at the roof of the car. Someone had spray painted there, in orange Day-Glow paint, a huge portrait of an erect penis rising from two monstrous testicles. Coon barely noticed it. He liked to daydream while riding the train, and already he was imagining himself being driven around in a Cadillac half a block long, giving orders over a phone in the back seat. He wanted a big apartment for his family uptown, and to have it furnished with the best. When Coon tried to imagine what "the best" was, though, he blanked, and eventually resolved to hire someone to furnish the apartment for him. "That's how they do it uptown," he said aloud.

Coon liked uptown New York, and he swore that's where he'd live when he grew up. Now he settled for walking the sidewalks in front of the fanciest buildings, daydreaming. There were even a few buildings where, by climbing the fire escapes or getting up on a roof, he could peek into the window and get a glimpse of the people who lived there. The train continued to rush over the tracks as he thought about his best find, a rooftop uptown with a skylight that looked down on an indoor swimming pool. Getting to this rooftop wasn't easy: it involved a few leaps and jumps that made even as accomplished a city athlete as Coon nervous. But once he got there he was glad he did it. Most of the time the pool was empty and there was no one to use the fancy lounge chairs spread around the tiled deck, or the three diving boards at one end of the pool, each a different height. Then Coon would just stare down at the blue water and daydream while he waited for the woman he had twice seen using the pool, hoping she would show up again.

She must have been, he thought, a model or an actress or something like that, because he had never seen a woman on the street who was so attractive. She had light blond hair, almost white, and skin that was tanned a golden brown. The first time he saw her she was wearing a one-piece white bathing suit, and she swam slowly and steadily back and forth across the length of the pool, lap after lap for almost an hour; then she got out, took a towel off the deck, and left. The second time, she had two children with her. One was a boy about the same age and build as Coon; the other was a girl a few years older. That time she was wearing a robe as she lay in a lounge chair and watched the children swim. It never occurred to Coon that she might be their mother until he heard the boy call to her in a frail, squeaky voice, and he heard the word *mother* float up to him dreamily, as if across a great distance; and still the relationship didn't sink in until much later. It didn't seem possible that she could be anyone's mother.

Coon was thinking hard about this when he felt a hand on his shoulder. At first he didn't respond. He thought he was on the roof, looking down at the pool, at the woman lying on a lounge chair. Then he felt himself being shaken.

He opened his eyes and saw a well-dressed man sitting alongside him.

"Are you all right?" the man asked. He was sitting sideways on the bench, looking at Coon. His right hand was on Coon's knee.

Coon sat up straight and edged away from him. "I'm okay," he said. "I didn't see you get on the train."

"I guess not," the man said. "You were sleeping."

Something about being asleep on the subway bothered Coon, and he resented it. "I wasn't sleeping."

"Oh," the man said, "okay."

Coon backed away another inch and looked hard at the stranger. He was wearing a three-piece, gray, pin-striped suit, without a wrinkle in it that Coon could notice. He had on a white shirt with a button-down collar, and a maroon tie with a fleur-de-lys pattern. His face was thin and clean-shaven, and he had big, dark eyes, with dark circles under them. The circles under his eyes made him look a little ragged, regardless of how well and neatly he was dressed.

"Why are you staring like that?" the man asked.

Coon said, "I'm not staring."

"Oh," the man said, and he turned away from Coon and sat back, stretching his arms out along the seat so that his forearm was behind Coon's neck.

Coon turned sideways in the seat. "You rich?" he asked.

The man smiled. "Why do you ask that?" he said. Then after a minute he added, "I'm certainly not poor."

"You're not rich!" Coon said. "Else you wouldn't be on the subway."

The man smiled again and looked as though he were impressed with Coon's observation. "What's your name?" he asked.

"Clay," Coon answered. "What's yours?"

"Talbot," the man said. "Everybody calls me Tal."

Coon nodded and Tal smiled again and ruffled Coon's hair in a friendly, fatherly way.

Coon resisted his first impulse to jump away from the stranger's hand. He wasn't sure whether or not this man was rich, but if he was rich, maybe there was something he could get from him. He let him ruffle his hair, and he didn't pull away when the stranger's hand rested for a moment on his head. "You really rich?"

Tal looked around the still empty car, and then moved closer to Coon. "Here," he said, pressing his lips together. He reached into the inside pocket of his jacket and came out with a crisp, new, hundred dollar bill. "Here," he said, and he offered the bill to Coon.

Coon didn't move.

"Go ahead," Tal said, and he waved the bill in front of Coon's eyes.

Coon scowled. "What do I have to do for it?"

Tal shook his head. "Nothing," he said. "Nothing at all."

Coon stared at him, trying to figure out what this man wanted. Tal's eyes were sunk deep beneath the ridge of his eyebrows, and, surrounded by dark sleep-circles, they looked

46

absolutely black. Coon started to reach for the bill, making only the slightest move with his hand. He looked at Tal's black eyes and saw the yellow light of the subway caught there, glittering. He took the bill and held it a moment, as if to give the man a chance to change his mind; then he pushed it deep in his pants pocket. Weakly he said, "Thank you."

"Good," Tal said. "That's a lot of money, you know?"

"I know!" Coon said, still nervous, but with some wonder in his voice.

"Good." Tal stood up in front of Coon. He was wearing brown loafers, polished to a bright shine. On one of them there was a smudge of something crusted and yellowish. Carefully, he took a handkerchief out of his pocket and rubbed at his shoe until the spot was gone. He folded the handkerchief and started to put it back in his pocket but then apparently thought better of it and dropped it on the floor. He kicked it under the seat. "I'm tired of riding this train," he said. His voice sounded sleepy.

"You sound tired," Coon said.

Tal nodded. "I can't get a good night's sleep anymore."

Coon stared up at Tal, and Tal looked back down at Coon. For a while they stayed like that, staring at each other like the strangers they were, trying to read each other's faces. Then the train slowed down for another station stop. "I'm going to get out here and take a cab," Tal said. "Do you want to come with me?"

"Where?" Coon asked.

"To where I live," Tal answered.

Coon shook his head, but it was only half-hearted. He didn't want to lose track of a man who gave away hundred dollar bills.

Tal yawned and rubbed his eyes. He seemed to pick up a little as the train came to a stop. "Come on," he said. "I've got a milk-shake machine in my apartment, and there might be some more of what you already got waiting for you there."

"Money?" Coon said.

Tal gestured with his eyebrows, as if to say, "sure thing!" Then the car door slid open, and Tal waited.

"Are you sure you're rich?" Coon said.

Tal nodded. "Come on," he said. "Let's go."

"Sure," Coon said. "I could use the money."

⋆   ⋆

From the outside, Coon had been disappointed with Tal's building. It was uptown, but it wasn't the fanciest part of uptown. Once inside, though, he wasn't disappointed at all. It was the biggest apartment he had ever seen, and it was carpeted from wall to wall with a rug that looked too white to walk on. In a corner of the apartment there was a grand piano, and all along the walls there were books and paintings and sculptures.

Coon had waited in the doorway as Tal entered the apartment.

"Come on," Tal said, and he gestured for Coon to join him on the couch.

On the way over, in the cab, Tal had said something about Coon's clothes, about having to get him a new wardrobe, and Coon had looked down and noticed how scruffy and dirty his sneakers were. Now he hesitated to walk on the white rug.

"Don't be nervous," Tal said. He joined Coon at the door and put his arm around Coon's shoulder, leading him into the living room.

"This is a nice place," Coon said.

"Thank you," Tal said. Then he stopped and yawned so loudly that it frightened Coon. "Excuse me." He took his closed fist away from his mouth, shook himself, and continued to show Coon into the apartment. "You know, you're not the first little friend I've had," he said. "Come here. I want to show you something."

Coon let himself be led into the bedroom, which, like the rest of the apartment, was carpeted in white. He sat down where he was told, on the edge of an oversized bed, on a white quilt, and waited while Tal took a box out of a dresser drawer.

Tal sat alongside Coon and held the box in his lap. "You know what's in here?"

Coon shook his head. It made him nervous to be in such a

48

fancy apartment, but he was truly curious now about Tal, about a man who could live in such a place. Coon had thought, from first meeting Tal on the subway, that he had some idea what the man wanted. But now, in the midst of such a clean and luxurious place, he wasn't sure.

Tal took the cover off the box. Inside there was a Polaroid camera and pictures of several boys, all around Coon's age.

"Who're they?" Coon asked.

Tal nodded once or twice, as if answering someone's question. Then he jerked back a little, as if a shiver had run through him. "What was that, Clay? What did you say?"

"I asked who they were," Coon said.

"Oh! They're my little friends. Whenever I make a new friend, I take his picture." He took out the Polaroid, leaned back and snapped a shot of Coon.

Coon smiled.

"That means you're one of my friends now," Tal said.

"Okay," Coon answered.

Then Tal leaned over and kissed him on the cheek.

Coon jerked away and fell back awkwardly on the bed, his head resting on a pillow. Tal leaned over him, holding the box in his lap. His eyes seemed to grow darker as Coon looked up at him.

Tal's breathing grew heavier and slower. "Don't be afraid of me," he said, and he smiled.

"I'm not afraid."

"Good. Good," Tal continued. "My father, you know, used to kiss me like that, just when I was your age. Every night, when he put me to bed."

As Coon watched, Tal smiled again, but this time his head jerked as he smiled and his black eyes blinked wildly.

"Let me show you something else." Tal picked himself up off the bed, sighing as he did so, as if it were a great effort. He replaced the box in the top drawer, and then he pulled the whole second drawer out of the dresser and placed it on the bed alongside Coon. It was filled with boys' clothing: there were several sets of socks, pants, briefs, T-shirts, shirts— everything but shoes. The clothes were all crumpled and stuffed into the drawer.

"These are some outfits," Tal said, "that I bought for my little friends." He took out a shirt and showed Coon the label. "See that," he said. "Only the best for my friends."

Coon nodded, though the label meant nothing to him.

"And here," Tal continued. He reached into the bottom of the drawer and felt around until he pulled out a couple of bright gold rings and shiny silver dollars.

Coon perked up at the sight of the rings and money. "What are they?" he asked.

"That's what my best friends get," he said. "Here," he added. "Look," and he handed Coon one of the rings so he could take a better look.

Coon saw that one side of the ring had diamonds embedded in it. "Gee," he said. "I bet this cost a lot of money."

Tal nodded. "That ring," he said, "cost several thousand dollars," and he gently took the ring out of Coon's hand.

"How much is several thousand dollars?" Coon asked.

Tal put the drawer back in its place.

Coon wondered why all the rings and clothes were in the drawer, and why the boys he bought them for weren't wearing them. "Hey," he said. "How come your friends aren't wearing those rings and stuff?"

Tal blinked a few times. He took a handkerchief out of his pants pocket and wiped his eyes. "Oh," he said, "they have lots of other rings and clothes. These are just what they've left behind. They're not using them just now."

"Oh," Coon said.

Tal sat close to Coon on the bed. "You see, I'm very good to my friends, Clay."

Coon nodded, and he didn't resist when Tal lifted him and then pressed him down on his stomach against the bed. Now he knew what Tal wanted—it was what he had guessed all along—and he felt almost glad that Tal was doing it, though it wasn't something he liked. This had happened to him before, when Virac, the old drunk who lived next door, had caught Coon trying to steal a radio out of his apartment. He too had done this to Coon, and said it was punishment for being a thief. Then over the next three months, till he moved away, he did it to Coon four more times, each time paying him five dollars and saying that he'd have him arrested for trying to steal his radio if he told. Coon never told. Now he remembered the hundred dollar bill in his pants pocket. He wanted to reach down and hold the money, but he'd have to wait till Tal was finished before he could get to it. Still, he knew the bill was there, and now he knew it was really his.

When Tal stopped he was breathing loudly, and he pulled away from Coon and sat on the edge of the bed. While Tal fixed himself up, Coon pulled his pants back on and straightened out his hair. Then he smiled at Tal, glad the worst part was over, and hoping that now Tal would give him something more.

"See," Tal said. He was almost whispering, and his head bobbed while he spoke. He seemed to be having a hard time keeping himself awake. "See," he said, barely audible, "now you're one of my best friends."

"Good," Coon said. He was eager for what would come next; but while he waited, Tal's eyes closed and his head fell to his chest. He made a snoring sound.

Coon shook Tal's arm. "Hey, Tal," he said. "You said you might have something more for me." Tal didn't wake. Coon shook him again. "Hey, Tal," he said.

When Coon saw that Tal wasn't going to wake up, he stood and quietly pulled out the drawer with the box and looked inside. Alongside the box there were stacks of coins, mostly silver dollars, but lots of other coins too, half dollars, quarters, foreign coins, subway tokens. Coon touched a few, looking furtively back at Tal as he did. Then he looked at the photos inside the box. There were six of them, each of a boy about his age, each taken in Tal's apartment. In the next drawer, Coon noticed there were six of everything: six pairs of pants, six silver dollars, six rings, and—something Tal hadn't shown him—six heavy gold necklaces. Coon started to open the next drawer, but Tal stopped snoring and pushed it closed before Coon could get a look inside. When he turned around Tal was looking at him. He looked like his father when he came home drunk. His mouth hung open and his eyes were dazed. "Are you okay?" Coon asked.

"You didn't take anything out of those drawers, did you Clay?" Tal asked in a whisper.

Coon shook his head.

Tal blinked several times and then he nodded. "Good, Clay. You don't want me to be severe with you. I can be very severe."

"I didn't take anything," Coon said.

"Good." Tal patted the bed alongside him. "Come sit by me."

Coon shook his head. "I have to get going. What about what you said? You said you'd have something for me."

"Do you have to go?" Tal asked.

"I have to be home for supper."

"Oh." Tal looked hard at Coon. "Well," he said, "you'll be back again, won't you Clay?"

Coon shrugged.

"Would you like one of those rings? One with the diamonds?"

"Sure!" Coon said. "I sure would!"

"Then you come back tomorrow," Tal said. "Come back and I'll have a ring for you, and maybe we'll buy you a new wardrobe. And . . . And . . ." Once again Tal's head started bobbing and dropping to his chest. His eyes closed. He was having a difficult time finishing his sentence. "And . . . they'll be . . . surprises . . . surprise . . ."

"But what about now!" Coon shouted.

Tal's head jerked back and his eyes opened. "Oh," he said. His arm moved as if it were something dead and heavy. He reached into his jacket pocket and pulled out a new silver dollar. "Here," he managed to say. "Here."

Coon scowled. He put the coin in his pocket, next to the hundred-dollar bill, and when he looked up Tal appeared to be sleeping again. "Tal?" Coon said. When Tal didn't answer, he reached for the bottom drawer, the drawer he hadn't yet seen, and started to pull it open slowly.

Tal's arm shot out and slammed the drawer closed. His voice boomed. "Don't make me angry!" he said. "I can be very severe, Clay. Do you hear me?"

Coon moved away. "I'm sorry Tal," he said. "I was just looking."

"I know," Tal said. He sighed and his voice turned sleepy again. "I know. Come back tomorrow and you'll get your reward." Then he laughed an odd, low laugh, and added in a whisper: "And don't show anyone the money, Clay. They'll take it away. You hear?"

Coon didn't need to be told. "I know," he said. "I won't."

Tal smiled weakly. "I just can't keep myself awake," he said, and in a moment his head had dropped to his chest and he was snoring again.

Coon's eyes moved back and forth from the drawer to the figure on the bed. Tal appeared to be sleeping soundly: he was sitting up and his chin was pressed flat against his chest. With every breath he took his head rose; then he'd exhale with a snort, and his head would drop and bob before rising again.

"Tal," Coon whispered.

Tal's head, eyes still closed, rose slowly and turned even more slowly to face Coon.

Coon backed out of the door. The man on the bed before him was still neatly dressed in a fine three-piece suit, but now his hair was messed up, and his face looked like a ghost's or a vampire's, the skin white and rubbery, the eyes so deep they looked like skull holes. The man looked dead: it was as if a corpse had sat up in its coffin, dressed in its best suit, and was looking at Coon.

Coon forgot about the rings, and the money and the gold necklaces. He backed out of the bedroom and ran out of the apartment.

★   ★

Coon was late. As he walked into the kitchen, his family was quiet. They were sitting around the table with dishes of soup in front of them. They had stopped eating.

"You'd better sit your ass down before this gets any colder," Alice said.

Coon sat at the table, in front of his spot.

"Go ahead," his mother said. She pointed to his plate.

Coon picked up his spoon and began eating. The room was small, and from where he sat Coon could feel the heat of the stove against his arm, and the thick smell of tomato soup drifted from a pot on one of the burners. Coon ate his soup slowly. His father wanted supper and his family waiting for him when he came home from work. That was a rule, and Coon was waiting to be yelled at.

"Where have you been?" his mother asked.

"Out," Coon answered.

"Out!" his father yelled. He slammed his fist against the table.

"I'm sorry," Coon said.

His father shook his head. He breathed heavily as he looked about the table: at his wife, who had her hair in curlers and in a pink and blue checked kerchief wrapped around her hair and tied in a big bow on top of her head; at the dark birthmark that masked his son's eyes; at his daughter, with her platinum and orange hair; at her blouse, which was ripped down the middle so that the insides of both breasts were exposed. He stared longest and hardest at Alice, and it was clear that he was too angry at her to have much left over for Coon.

"Look at this," he said at last. "Look at this," he repeated, gesturing with his hand. "My own private, goddamned freak show." Then he pushed his chair back and left the table.

Coon watched him through the window as he walked out of the apartment and up to the street.

"Fuck him," Alice said, once he was gone.

"Don't you talk that way," her mother said.

"Fuck you too," Alice said, and she got up and stormed away to her room.

"See what you did," his mother said to Coon. She was resting her head in the palms of both hands and rocking it from side to side as she looked down at her soup.

Coon turned away from the table and found himself looking at his reflection in the mirror by the stove. Behind him he saw his mother. With her fingertips, she was pulling the skin back from her eyes and so distorting her face she looked monstrous. Coon tried to imagine in his mother's place the beautiful woman from uptown, the woman from the swimming pool who was some other boy's mother. He couldn't. So he squinted until she disappeared. Then he looked at himself looking at himself, and he squinted harder, trying to make his mask disappear. Soon his eyes closed, and then he thought of

Tal, and he reached into his pocket to feel the silver dollar and the hundred dollar bill.

"Well," his mother said softly, "are you going to tell me where you were?"

Coon didn't answer. He was busy dreaming of the diamond-studded rings in Tal's drawer, of the grand piano in the huge, white-carpeted apartment, and of all the fine clothes and all the money he could get from Tal. He didn't even hear his mother's question. It was as if he had already gone to see Tal. It was as if he were already long gone.

PEACE,
BROTHER

———————————

I couldn't sleep. For one thing, a church was on fire outside my back window. The night was moonless, and the attic where I kept my bed had no lights. Lying on my side, naked under a white sheet, I looked out the low window, across two vacant lots, and watched the church burn. First there had been sirens and men shouting, but now everything was quiet except for the sound of the fire. Flames shot out of windows and exploded through big holes in the roof. In their light, I could see several red fire trucks parked in a semicircle, men dressed in black milling around the trucks. The fire lit up my attic too, casting a wavering red glow over bare wood, lighting up knot holes through which the wind blew. I rearranged my pillow and watched the long red arms of flame reach out of the bell tower and grasp at the slender crucifix atop the church steeple. Then the fire erupted through the right side of the roof in a bright flash and the bell tower tilted.

I sat up as firemen scurried behind trucks. One of the bells fell to the pavement and a single note tolled and reverberated before giving way to the crackle of flames. I propped open the window with a stick, and knelt on the rough wooden floorboards, my elbows resting on the windowsill. Through that summer night, I watched the fire. By the time the last truck left, the church was reduced to rubble and the sun was just coming up over the mountains. All over town, my friends were getting out of bed. In the last two weeks more than twenty of us had been drafted. Today we were going to Albany to take our physicals.

Downstairs, a Doors tune came on, loud, and lasted maybe four bars before Bill pulled the plug out of the wall, which was how he turned off the radio alarm every morning. Bill was a dropout, as were most of my friends—Whitethorn, New York, being more of an artist's colony than a town. Mostly, we hung out and did drugs and had a good time. Bill was fifteen years older than me and the rest of my friends. We were college dropouts; Bill had left a high-paying job. He had also left his wife and kid. Now he painted. Sometimes. Most of the time he was stoned and hanging out with Betty—his girlfriend who was my age.

I crawled to a place in the room where the peaked roof met the attic floor. It was a tight squeeze, but I wedged my head into the corner and pushed aside a loose floorboard, enabling me to look down through a hole in the ceiling into Bill's room. Bill was sitting on the edge of his bed, staring into the empty kitchen, a sheet wrapped around his shoulders. "Hey, man," I said. "What's the time?"

Bill answered without looking up. "We're going to have to fix that hole."

"Why? I like it."

He fell back on the bed and looked up at me. "You don't have a thing to worry about, Joe. You're too weird for the Army."

"I hope. What's the time?"

He reached under the bed and plugged in the clock radio. "Six-thirty, give or take."

"Bus leaves at eight."

"Sally up there?"

I shook my head and crawled back from the hole before he could ask me anything more about Sally.

A pair of skimpy red panties lay on a chair next to the window. I looked at them warily. For the past two weeks, a few guys had been drafted every day. They'd come running into the Homestead—a bar where we spent our time playing chess, talking politics, drinking wine and beer—waving their official government envelopes. We were, every one of us, opposed to the Vietnam war. We went as a group, as the Whitethorn contingent, to peace marches in Washington and New York. We were going to end the war in Vietnam on the streets of the U.S. We weren't going. No way. As each draft notice came, we made our plans. We'd blow them away in Albany. Some of us decided on drugs designed to screw up the physical, but most were going to be actors for a day, playing out deranged personalities. I was supposed to show up in women's underwear. That, I had been told, was sure to get me out. All I had to do was play it absolutely straight—normal all the way. Then, when I got undressed, pretend I found nothing shocking in what I was wearing and argue for my God-given American right to go around in any underwear I damn well chose. Now, the moment having arrived to actually put the stuff on, I hesitated.

This was a hard thing to do. Until the age of fifteen, I had been an altar boy at St. Francis's in Brooklyn. I came from an Italian-American family, where the men didn't wear women's undergarments—or if they did, no one knew about it. My father was a doctor and a member of the Knights of Columbus. My mother was a nurse. They had met in the Pacific during the war, married when they came home, and last month they celebrated their twenty-fifth anniversary. They had four daughters and one son—me. I wasn't supposed to go around in red panties.

Outside, I heard someone playing blues harp. I looked out the window and saw Dave coming up the street with Skip and Harper. Dave, the only bona fide madman among us, was dressed neatly in sandals, khaki slacks, and a madras shirt. His shoulder-length hair was pulled back into a neat ponytail.

Dave had a face that reminded me of Howdy Doody, with his fat, freckled cheeks and constant, inane smile. For reasons no one could manage to get out of him, he wanted to go to Vietnam. All we could figure out was that it had something to do with alchemy—Dave's great passion. He believed himself a magician, an alchemist, descended, he claimed, from one of the Magi who followed the star to Bethlehem. We weren't worried about the Army taking Dave away.

Harper, an ex-medical student, nodded his head to Skip's harmonica playing. He was wearing a surgical cap and gown, and already had a white face mask tied over his mouth and nose. He was going to claim to be afraid of foreign germs. There didn't seem to be anything unusual in Skip's appearance. He was wearing torn jeans and a tie-dyed T-shirt, scraggly brown hair down to the middle of his back, wire-rimmed glasses. Then I noticed the bright red, high intensity reading light strapped to his belt and remembered that he planned to refuse to walk from one room to another without extending the telescoping neck of the reading light and scanning the doorway for harmful rays. He hoped the Army would see this as hopelessly paranoid-schizophrenic behavior. I looked one more time at the red panties and ran quickly through my options: go to Canada and live there, perhaps, for the rest of my life; go to jail for at least a few years; go to Albany for a day in women's underwear.

I put on the panties. When I looked at myself in the mirror by my bed, I blushed. I was a smooth-skinned boy with straight, light brown hair that reached down to my shoulders. My blush, though, resulted more from a memory than my appearance. Once, when I was a boy, my parents were working in the yard and I was alone in their bedroom, looking through their drawers. I had found my mother's girdle and, not really thinking about what I was doing, I had undressed and put it on. Then I heard my father come into the house, and I was instantly and terribly afraid he'd catch me wearing my mother's underwear. I didn't get caught, but I was so ashamed of myself that for days after I walked around moody and tearful—afraid I was some kind of a pervert my parents would one day have to deny having raised.

Below me I heard Bill open the front door, and then the sound of Skip's harmonica playing came into the apartment. I pulled on my sneakers, my patched-up jeans, and my best green T-shirt. I went down to meet the boys.

Bill sat at our flimsy, Formica table with his standard breakfast in front of him: a cup of black, instant coffee and a Honey Bee doughnut. He had pushed last night's frozen dinner trays aside. I saluted Bill and started out the door with Skip and the others.

Bill said, "Don't let them scare you." He leaned back in his chair.

"We won't," I said. "We'll be cool."

Skip held two fingers up in a v, flashing Bill the peace sign. He said, "Peace, brother."

I lived about half a mile from the bus station, and the streets at that hour were empty. Whitethorn was settled in the seventeenth century by Dutch Huguenots, and some of their stone houses still stood along the streets on the way to the Greyhound station. The town kept them up as tourist attractions.

I had just told Skip about how the church looked when it was on fire last night, and he pointed at a stone house we were passing. "They should make 'em like that," he said. "Those mothers'll never burn."

"Yeah," I agreed. "That's why we need to get back to nature."

Harper was listening. He flipped his mask down and said, "Right on, brothers. Tell it like it is."

We all felt good then. There were trees along the street and they were filled with birds singing. I felt full of energy and alive, and for the rest of the walk I forgot I was wearing red panties under my jeans.

When we reached the Greyhound station, the bus to Albany was in the lot, waiting to load. Scores of young men were on the loading platform laughing and talking loudly. As we came into their sight, dozens of our friends called out to us.

Inside the terminal—which was actually a soda fountain with part of the counter reserved for selling bus tickets—a bunch of guys were sitting around drinking coffee. I paid for a round-trip ticket and ordered a cup of coffee to go. Skip did the same, and we went outside to sit on the platform.

A guy named Howard—we called him the Ironman, because he worked out with weights—was putting on a show in front of the platform. He had a red cap on, and books by Marx and Chairman Mao under his arms. As we all watched and listened, he read from the books, shouting and gesticulating. Then he took off his shoe and began screaming, "We will bury you!"

"He's a pisser," Skip said.

I nodded. We had about five minutes until loading. I was getting nervous again.

"You okay?"

"I'm cool."

"What about you and Sally? I don't see you guys hanging out like you used to."

"It's been a drag," I said, "since she had the abortion."

"When was that?" Skip put his coffee down. "I didn't know she was pregnant."

"She's not, anymore."

"I know. But I mean, I didn't know she had gotten pregnant."

"We didn't announce it," I said. "It was a drag. A real drag."

"Yeah," Skip said. "I can dig it. So you didn't want to get married?"

"I didn't." I hesitated, then shook my head—as if I had briefly reconsidered. "She did, though. She did if I wanted to. But I didn't, you know, so we went down to Pelham . . ." I shrugged.

"Well, that's cool," Skip said. "That's groovy. So Sally's mind's messed up?"

"No," I said. "Sally's just fine."

Skip was staring at me, like he was trying to puzzle out my meaning; but then the bus doors opened and everybody started moving.

Skip and I sat together on the bus. We were in the back and Dave and Harper and the rest of the Whitethorn contingent were seated all around us. Somebody started chanting, "Hell no, we won't go!" and everyone picked it up. We kept at it until the driver stopped and told us he had a hangover, so if we didn't mind . . . That made us laugh. We thought the driver was cool, and we quit chanting.

"The dude's groovy," Skip said.

"Right on," I answered.

"So listen," Skip said. "So what you're saying is, you're like the one's messed up, right?"

I said, "Listen, man. I really don't want to talk about it."

"That's cool." He patted me on the knee.

I didn't want to start talking about Sally and the abortion because I'd been a mess ever since the whole thing happened. First of all, since we came back, I hadn't been able to have sex with her. I'd just lie there and nothing would happen. I'd feel more like crying than touching. Then the dreams started. They were strange, but they weren't hard to figure out. In one of them, there was a baby in a file cabinet, and I kept trying to push the baby's head down into a file folder, so I could close the drawer; but it kept sticking up, and I couldn't close the file cabinet and get on with my business. Strange, but not hard to figure. That was only one dream, but there were lots of them I could remember. Pretty soon, I was killing babies or finding dead babies every night in my dreams; and during the day I was always arguing with myself about whether or not I did the right thing. It was hard. I wasn't eating right. I was nervous a lot. But Sally was cool about it. As far as I could see, it didn't bother her at all. I wasn't being cool. No way. I was freaked out.

Alongside me, Skip had fallen asleep. The bus had settled into a low, rumbling quiet that was the sound of the engines and the wheels over the Thruway and guys talking softly to their friends. Someone had lit an incense stick, and its sweet smell filled the bus. There were No Smoking signs at the front and back of the coach, but the driver was letting it pass. The smell of incense, as always, reminded me of when I was an altar boy—when I would swing the censor during Mass, dispensing that same sickly sweet smell through the cavernous church. St. Francis was one of the old, huge buildings, constructed entirely, it seemed, of gold and marble. It was a beautiful place, with ceilings so high it hurt my neck to look up to

the top of them. Statues, paintings, stained glass windows—
the whole works. My memories of St. Francis were good ones.
It was a wonderful place to be alone, and its atmosphere of
great stillness—in which every move anyone made echoed—
was a part of me. It was locked up in my head and the smell of
incense was only one of several keys.

When we pulled into Albany, the energy level on the bus
started rising. The sleepers awoke; the talk started getting
loud. Guys rehearsed their acts, getting into character. Skip
was tapping his foot so hard when the bus finally stopped, our
seat shook.

"All right!" the bus driver yelled. "This is it." He hunkered
down and pointed out the window. "That's the building right
up the block."

Skip said, "Hey man. You think I ought to get into this
right away? You know, scan the bus door on the way out?" He
jumped up and looked out the window. "Oh shit, man. I can
see two doorways from here."

I said, "Just be cool, man. Do your thing."

Skip nodded, sobered by my advice. On the way out of the
bus, he stopped at the door, but the guy behind him pushed
him through before he ever got a hand on his reading light.
On the street, he turned and yelled, to no one in particular,
"My nuclon scan!"

I laughed and touched his arm. He was sweating. He pulled
his arm away. "I can't," he said, "traverse a terrestrial plain
without doing a nuclon scan. It's dangerous."

"Skip," I said. But Skip scowled at me as if I were a fool. He
returned to the bus after everyone was off and while the
driver watched, he pulled out his reading light, switched it on,
and carefully scanned the doorway. When he finished, he
walked by me as if I weren't there.

I looked up to the driver, who was looking back at me.
"That's a class act," he said. He was a short guy with a beer
belly. "Next to the two guys who showed up naked, that's the
best act I've seen. What about you?" he asked. "You going, or
you one of these peace freaks?"

"Peace freak," I said.

He sneered and shook his head and closed the door.

When I stepped into the street, Skip was already scanning the entrance to the recruiting center. A man in uniform was watching him, asking loudly what the hell he was doing. Skip ignored him. Then the guy started screaming, and I could tell they weren't going to make this easy on us.

Inside, the recruiting center looked like a warehouse and felt like a train station. Guys in uniform were leading lines of young men through a massive lobby into scores of smaller rooms. I was directed to a place that looked like a college classroom—rows of chairs neatly lined up in front of a desk—and there I found the rest of the guys from the bus. My spirits rose when I saw my friends, and I went and took a seat alongside Harper.

Harper was already sweating through his gown, and his eyes swung back and forth nervously over his white face mask. "Where's Skip?" he asked, as if I had abandoned him someplace where he might be in danger.

"He was doing his scanning thing at the entrance."

"Oh, Christ," Harper said. "I know I'm not going to get through this."

I said, "Just be cool, Harper. Do your thing."

Harper seemed to be reassured by this. He nodded, sat up straight, and turned to the front of the room. I watched the door, but Skip never made it. Dave was sitting quietly in the front of the class, looking like a kid at Sunday School. He had his hands folded on the desk as he smiled at a middle-aged man in uniform who had just walked through the door and positioned himself behind the desk.

The man inside the uniform was skinny and frail. He leaned forward, put his hands on the desk, and said, "Men—"

Someone found this funny and began to laugh. Then someone else started singing the Hari Krishna song from *Hair*, and then we were all singing it. The frail soldier shouted for us to stop, but we didn't. He left and was replaced by three more soldiers, one of whom looked angry. The angry one stepped to the front of the room and said, "Cut the shit, assholes!" and there was something in his tone of voice that stopped us cold. We shut up. He pointed to Harper and said to one of the men by the door, "Get that clown out of here."

Harper said, "What? What's wrong? What's the problem?" and kept protesting that way while he was led out of the room. Then they broke all of us up and took us off in different directions.

One of the first places I went was for a hearing test. I sat in a big box that looked like a refrigerator. I had a set of earphones on, and there was a green button and a blue button on a panel in front of me. Every time I heard a noise in my right ear, I was supposed to hit the green button; in my left ear, the blue button. For a while, there was just silence. Then the first high-pitched tone sounded in my right ear. I hit the green button. Next, a lower pitch, again in my right ear. I hit the green button again. There were several more notes, in varying pitches, all in my right ear; and I hit the green button again and again. Several times there were long intervals between notes, and I was beginning to worry that there might be some problem with the hearing in my left ear, when I at last heard a high-pitched note sounded there. I didn't hit the blue button. The note sounded again, and again I didn't hit the button. They sounded a whole range of notes, all of which I pretended not to hear. Finally, they returned to the right ear and I happily hit the green button.

When I came out of the refrigerator, a fat man in a white smock was waiting for me. He shined a light in my left ear and asked, "You have any problem with the hearing in this ear?" "Yes," I said. "I don't hear so well in that ear."

He leaned close, so that his forehead was touching my temple, and shouted, "That's too bad!"

When I jumped and grabbed my ear, he smirked, checked his clipboard and pointed me in the right direction for the next test.

By midafternoon, I still hadn't been asked to take off my clothes. I learned—while having my eyes examined—that they wanted to keep our guys separate, and so they had changed the order of the exams. So far, I figured I was a solid 1A, and if I didn't make the underwear trip work, I'd be in big trouble. I was getting worried. Skip and Harper had disappeared. I hadn't even seen them in passing. But it seemed every time I crossed the lobby, I'd see Dave and he'd give me the thumbs-up sign and wink at me. I pictured myself marching through a rice paddy in Vietnam with Dave at the point. I had seen so much of the Vietnam war on television and in pictures that this wasn't at all hard for me to visualize.

While I was waiting for one more test in what was beginning to seem like an endless series of tests, a handsome, casually dressed older man approached the line and asked, "Which of you is Joseph Famiglia?" I didn't answer immediately. The man looked like Robert Young from *Father Knows Best*. He had soft, blue eyes and a full head of hair that was gray only at the temples, and he carried a big meerschaum pipe in his right hand. He lifted the pipe to his mouth. I said, "I am, sir." As soon as I said it, he smiled; and I wondered what in God's name had possessed me to say *sir*.

He put his arm around my shoulder and led me out of the line. I went with him, unquestioningly, to a small office where he pulled up a chair alongside his desk and motioned for me to sit down. He fell back into a big leather recliner that looked like it belonged in someone's living room. Framed diplomas announcing degrees in medicine and psychiatry were positioned on the wall above his chair. A folder lay open on a messy ink blotter in front of him, and in it I could see a bunch of papers with my name atop them. "I'm Jay Biggs," he said. "Your father might have mentioned the name to you."

I shook my head. "You know my father?"

He pointed at me. "Your father's a good man. He ever tell you about Corregidor?"

"Corregidor?"

"Corregidor was a hellhole. Our boys were slaughtered there. Mike and I—your father and I—were with the first medical team in." He shook his head. "Son," he said. "You wouldn't believe the things we saw."

I didn't know what to say in response to that, and then, as I looked at him, the man's eyes grew watery. I was afraid he was going to cry if I didn't say something soon. "Gee," I said. "That sounds terrible."

It was strange in that office. I felt as though I had walked into a time warp, and a mysterious force was making me behave like a teenager in a fifties situation comedy.

We looked at each other awkwardly for a few more moments, and then he stood and put his arm around my shoulder again, and led me to the door. "Well," he said, "it's your turn now, you boys. I just wanted to tell you that I knew your father, and that I'm proud to have served with him."

I nodded awkwardly and then heard myself say, "Yes, sir. I'll be sure to tell him."

He patted me on the back and then, as if the idea just came to him, he said, "Let me take you over, so you don't have to wait in line again."

I protested, politely, but he led me past the line I had been waiting on and into a room where a half dozen guys were lined up in front of a man with a clear plastic glove on one hand. My father's war buddy said, "Al, take good care of this boy. I served with his father." Then he patted me on the back and left the room, closing the door behind him with a click.

Al said, "Okay, men. Drop your pants."

I hesitated for only a second before I unclipped my belt buckle and let my pants drop to the floor.

"Jesus Christ," Al said. He looked at me as if I were dirty and then left the room. The other guys in line checked me out and started laughing. One of them asked, "You really a fag, or you just want out?"

I didn't get a chance to answer before Al returned with the guy who had shut us all up this morning. Now he looked even angrier. "All right, faggot," he said. "Let's go."

I bent down to pick up my pants.

"Leave them off! Carry them over your arm!"

I did as he said. When we walked out the door, everybody in the line laughed at me, and someone made an obscene kissing sound.

Jay Biggs could hardly have had time to get settled in his chair before I was standing in front of him again—this time in red panties. When I first came through the door, he seemed confused. He looked me in the eye, as if to ask what the problem was. Then he looked lower. "Sergeant," he said. "Just leave him here."

The sergeant said, "I'll wait outside the door."

Jay Biggs motioned for me to put my pants on, which I did with great relief.

"Do you have a problem, Joe?" he asked.

The answer to his question came to mind immediately. Yes,

I wanted to say. Vietnam is my problem. But the words stuck in my throat, because Jay Biggs had the power to send me to Vietnam if he thought I was faking it. I said, "I'm homosexual. I'm a transvestite. I always dress like this."

Jay watched me hard. My eyes were watery, but I didn't think he could notice. I kept telling myself not to screw up, not to start crying like a baby—which is what I felt welling up inside me. One part of me wanted to beg him not tell my father about this, but another part of me was ashamed at the childishness of the thought. I tapped my foot to keep my whole body from shaking.

"But you don't want to go to Vietnam," he said. "You don't want to fight for your country." He sounded as though he had said the same words a thousand times before to a thousand other young men. He sounded tired.

"That's not true," I said. "I'd love to go to Vietnam." I raised my eyebrows. "All those boys. I'd just love it."

He lowered his eyes and opened my file. He checked a few boxes, signed his name a few times and then left the room. A minute later, the sergeant returned. He said, "Let's go," and I followed him through the lobby and out into the street. "Take the next bus," he said, "back to wherever you came from. We don't need scum like you." He turned and walked back into the building. I watched him walk away from me and noticed for the first time a jagged scar that came up out of the collar of his uniform and disappeared into his hairline.

I was halfway to the bus station before the pleasant realization sunk in that at least it was over. I had played my act for the Army and won my 4F. I guessed that Skip and Harper had been tossed out earlier, and that was why I hadn't seen them all day. In the bus terminal, I found the men's room first thing. I locked myself in a stall and took off the red panties. When I came out, I saw Dave sitting on a bench, on the loading platform. I sat next to him, and he seemed glad to see me.

"How'd it go?" he asked.

"Groovy," I said. "I got what I wanted. What about you?"

"Bummed out, man. They had my records from Bellevue." He made a face. "They said they were sorry, though. They wished everybody had my desire."

"Dave, man. I really don't get why you wanted to go."

Dave looked at me thoughtfully. "I guess I can tell you now. It's the fire, man. You ever see the fire in Vietnam? I saw a whole mountain burning. It's something, man. It's the biggest fire I ever seen."

I didn't get it. "What's that got to do with anything?"

"Fire, man. Fire's the element that transmutes matter. A fire like that, man . . ."

Dave was looking at me as though I had to be a simpleton not to understand what he was getting at. I said, "If it's fire you want, Dave, why don't you go to Watts, or Newark, or Harlem? They're burning those places to the ground."

"No way," Dave said. "A guy in Newark hit me on the head with a rock, man, and I wasn't even doing anything. I'm scared of those black guys, man."

For the first time since I'd known him, I realized just how crazy Dave really was. I let the subject drop, and when the bus came, I tried to sit away from him; but he followed me and sat beside me. I was exhausted. I put my seat back and closed my eyes.

Dave was quiet for a while before he started to whistle. Then he said, "How's Sally doing, man."

"Fine," I said.

He said, "You're really lucky to have a girlfriend like Sally. She's really nice."

I nodded. I hadn't seen Sally in weeks. The last time I was with her, we had lain together on the old railroad tracks and tossed rocks into the river, both of us knowing that things had changed. I didn't want to touch her. I didn't even want to be with her.

Dave said something else, which I barely heard, and then I fell asleep. When I woke, we were in Whitethorn and Dave was shaking me. We walked together to my house, and by the time Dave gave me the peace sign and continued on to his own place, it was almost dark.

When I stepped into my apartment, the place reeked of grass. Bill's ex-wife was suing him for child support, and there were legal papers spread out all over the table—over the frozen food trays and the coffee cups and the doughnut crumbs. Bill was crashed out in his room, a nickel bag of grass on the floor beside his bed. He was lying on his back with his mouth open, and he looked old in the dim light. While I watched, he opened his mouth wide and gasped, as if he were drowning.

I walked quietly past him and went up to the attic, where I got out of my clothes. I lay down on my bed, thinking I would fall asleep immediately, but I didn't. I lay there for a few minutes, and then I got up and looked out the window. In the rubble of the church fire, I saw two kids playing. They couldn't have been more than seven or eight, and they were both filthy, covered with soot and ash. I couldn't tell what game it was they were playing, and I doubted that they knew. They were just playing, having a good time, shouting and jumping up and down. I knew it had to be dangerous doing what they were doing. The church probably had a basement, and they risked falling into it. There had to be nails sticking up and broken things with sharp edges. I should have done something. I should have gone down and made them stop playing. But I just stood there and watched them. I stood still in my attic and watched those kids playing in the rubble until it was too dark to see anything at all.

THIS
WORLD
THAT
WORLD

Beyond a double-insulated bay window that took up most of the kitchen wall, the pale winter sun baked a snow crust to a glaze. Mia touched her finger to the warm glass. In front of her, on the kitchen table, eggs, bacon, and home fries crowded an aqua blue plate. A cup of café au lait steamed alongside the plate. This was Sunday morning, two days after Mia's eighteenth birthday. Janice, Mia's mother, poured herself a cup of black coffee at the kitchen counter. With her free hand, she jotted something onto a yellow legal pad.

Mia sipped her coffee and turned away from the wrinkled green robe that covered her mother's broad back. Friday, after school, before going out for her birthday dinner with Janice, she had been prowling around in the basement and found an old photo album in a taped-up cardboard box. The first few pages held pictures of her mother and father from early in their marriage, long before Mia was born, long before

73

they divorced when Mia was six years old. She sat down on the damp concrete floor and flipped through the pictures, only mildly interested. The photos were in no particular order. One group was shots of Janice's graduation from divinity school, and another was of her first sermon at the Unitarian congregation where she was minister. These were all from long after the divorce. Then another bunch jumped back in time, again, to a date before Mia was born. Even then, her mother had been a big woman, wide-shouldered, big-hipped, with a ramrod straight posture that made her an imposing figure. She made men nervous, because she looked big enough to knock most of them on their behinds should she want to, and often enough she looked like she wanted to. Mia was her mother's anatomical opposite, a small-boned waif of a girl with fine blond hair, sharp delicate features, and big eyes.

As she turned the pages of the album, Mia paused longest over the pictures of her father. She had just seen him last weekend, and it had been a good visit, as usual, even though the girlfriend who was living with him now was half his age and one-third his IQ. In the airport lounge—they had left Lois in the outer-terminal gift shop, giggling over the racy greeting cards—she had leaned her head against her father's arm and he had patted her gently on the shoulder. Just before she boarded the plane, she said to him, "Thank God Lois is pretty." He smiled and winked at her, and kissed her on the cheek before leaving. Mia watched him walk away. His clothes were too tight for a man his age—they accentuated the bulges in his waist and thighs—and, as always, as she had told him several times, his toupee looked silly.

In these old pictures, though, he was handsome. She turned the page and suddenly the pictures were black and white. This was someplace else. Even with the uniforms, and the men in foxholes, it still took Mia a minute to realize these were pictures from Korea. The Korean War was history to her; and though she knew her father had fought, that part of his past had never been real to her until she turned the page.

Most of the pictures were of tough, stubble-faced men she had never seen before, but in some of the pictures her father turned up, much younger than she had ever seen him, sometimes bare-chested, sometimes arm-in-arm with other young,

74

rugged-looking men. In one of the pictures her father was between two other men looking down into a ditch at decapitated
bodies. Two of the men looking into the ditch appeared solemn, but her father seemed to be upset. He looked as though
he were frightened. His face was tight and his lips were pressed
together. He looked as though he were poised to jump, as if
he feared that the two headless men might leap up at him.
The picture made her want to reach out and touch the young
man who used to be her father, to comfort him.

When Mia closed the album, she had made a decision. For
a long time—as long as she could remember (and every time
she got angry with her mother)—she had considered going to
live with her father. Now that she would be starting college in
the fall, going off on her own, she decided she wanted to
spend this last summer with him. She wanted to know him
better. She had a right.

Now all she had to do was tell her mother.

"Mom?" she asked. "What's that you're writing?"

Her mother turned from the counter with the coffee in one
hand and the yellow pad in the other. "You haven't eaten a
bite!" she said, looking at Mia's plate as if something there
amazed her.

Mia snapped off the end of a strip of bacon and popped it
into her mouth.

Janice sat across from Mia and placed her yellow pad next
to a lightly buttered slice of wheat toast.

Mia said, "Is that all you're eating?"

Janice looked at the toast thoughtfully. She said, "I'm getting fat." Then added, "Mia? I ask you: Does God care about
you and me?"

"You're the minister."

"I want your opinion."

"I don't know. Why?"

"Well, you know . . ." Janice went to the cupboard and
brought back a box of Melba toast. She had finished off the
wheat toast in a few bites. "That's the question." She buttered
the crisp surface of the bread. "That's what I'm wondering
about in this talk—if I finish it."

Mia checked the clock over the sink. "You have a couple of
hours yet. Anyway. I wanted to talk to you about something."

Janice nodded. "What I'm going to say is this: The God who made us, we say, is a force, like love or light—not something that can make it rain or save you from cancer. I mean, I'm simplifying things, but what I'm getting at in this sermon is: Isn't it an arrogant thing to believe God is a force but *we* have consciousness? Doesn't it mean that we can know the world in some ways that God can't? You see what I'm saying? God can't care about us because God's a force. But *we* can care. Isn't that smug? Doesn't that make us better than God? Do you see what I mean?"

Mia shook her head. "What? Maybe there is a God who can make it rain or save us from cancer?"

Janice shrugged.

"Isn't that, like, what everybody else believes? I mean, isn't that, like, normal religion?"

Janice smiled. "Yeah. But it's going to blow my congregation away." She found this so funny that she laughed and slapped the table.

Mia's plate rattled. She said, "That's good Mom, but listen . . . I think I want to stay with Dad this summer."

Janice's smile disappeared. "Honey," she said, "you just saw him last weekend. I'd think that would last you. Didn't you say he was living with some bimbo?"

"I didn't say anything like that. I said she was dumb."

"Oh. Excuse me. But now you want to spend the summer with him. This last, special summer before you go off to college." Janice looked down at the yellow pad and up at the clock. "Can this wait, Mia? Do we have to go over this right now? Right before my talk?"

"We don't have to go over anything." Mia spoke softly, as she usually did when her mother was angry. She said, "I just wanted you to know what I decided."

Janice's face seemed to contract, to tighten. "Okay. You've decided you want to go visit your father again. You've told me. Now I know."

Mia shook her head. "You're saying visit, Mom. I didn't say that. I said for the summer. I want to go live with him and Lois for the summer."

Janice yelled, "What do you mean, live with?" She slapped the table. "You mean, move into his house? Move all your stuff," she gestured toward Mia's bedroom, "into his house? You want to stay there?" She said these things as if they were utter absurdities, total impossibilities.

Mia nodded.

Janice didn't say anything, but her hand closed into a fist and after a second she banged the table so hard that Mia's plate jumped. A few seconds later she pounded the table again. This time the glass top rattled off the crystal sugar jar and broke neatly into two pieces when it hit the floor.

Mia bent to pick up one of the pieces. She felt light-headed. Her hand was shaking, and when she picked up the crystal, she cut her thumb. She closed her hand into a fist to hide the cut.

Janice left the table and stood by the counter. "You mean to tell me," she said, reaching her hand out toward Mia, "that that drunken, womanizing man who walked out on us when you were six years old, left me to raise you all these years by myself . . . and now, now when you're old enough to be no trouble . . ." The reasonable tone left her voice, and her face crumpled. "Now . . . when your company's a pleasure . . . You mean to tell me . . ." She was biting her lip, trying, apparently, not to lose her composure entirely.

Mia turned away from her mother and rested her head against the bay window. She felt hot and sick, as if she might throw up. She tried breathing deeply and evenly. Then, in a minute, she felt her mother's hand on her shoulder.

Janice's tone had suddenly changed. "What did you do?" She held her hand by the wrist.

Mia saw the blood dripping onto the table. She unclenched her fist and looked at the cut on her thumb. It didn't look very deep, but it was still bleeding.

"Christ." Janice put her arm around Mia's waist and walked her to the bathroom.

Mia saw her reflection in the bathroom mirror. Her face was pale and white. She had short, blond hair cut in an uneven bob. It was tousled and messy and looked like a rumpled hat sitting crookedly on her head. She straightened out her hair with her good hand while her mother ran her cut thumb under the water and put on iodine and a Band-Aid.

When Janice was done, they stood alongside each other

awkwardly. Mia started to say, "I'm sorry if I've hurt your feelings," but she didn't get any further than "I'm sorry" before she started crying.

Janice held her in her arms and patted her back. "Come on," she said. "Let's go for one of our walks."

"I only—"

"Wait. Let's wait."

"What about your talk?"

Janice waved off her concern. "I can wing it with what I've got." She steered her by the shoulders to the hall closet where they put on boots and coats.

Outside, they tracked through the crusty snow to a path that led into the woods. They both knew the path well: it cut through a few acres of woods to the main road, where there was a small grocery store. Mia and Janice walked side by side until they were out of sight of any house. Then Janice said, "Well, do you feel like you can talk now?"

Mia nodded.

"I'm sorry I exploded," she said. "That was very bad of me."

"No," Mia said. "You've got a right."

Janice said, "That's true." Ahead of her, where the path merged with a trail from another development, the snow disappeared and was replaced by frozen mud. "Looks like a highway back here." She pointed at all the boot and shoe prints in the mud.

"Kids come back here to get away from their homes."

Janice walked along the side of the path, avoiding the sharp ridges of dirt. She was wearing a heavy coat, and she pulled the collar up around her neck. "I really don't understand," she said. "If I had what you kids have when I was growing up, I wouldn't be tracking out into the woods to socialize."

Mia said, "Didn't you ever want to get away from your parents?" Then she corrected herself. "Your mother, I mean."

Janice stopped to rest. They had reached a small clearing. "My mother worked twelve hours a day. When I saw her, I certainly didn't want to get away."

"I can understand," Mia said, sharply. She looked around at the muddy floor of the clearing. Beer cans were scattered around the trees, along with muddy cigarette butts and empty cigarette packs and empty packs of rolling papers. "I remember coming out here to smoke a cigarette with Larkin when I was a kid."

"You didn't! You and Larkin Sheehy? I don't believe it."

"That's what kids do." She pointed to one of the trees. "They sit down by a tree trunk and smoke cigarettes."

Janice picked up a muddy beer can. "And drink beer." She nodded toward an empty pack of rolling papers. "And smoke marijuana. You never did *that*, did you?"

Mia made a face. "What do you think, Mom? I'm some kind of angel?" She shook her head. When she breathed out, she could see her breath flying away from her, first in a stream, then in a small cloud. She continued, "I haven't hung out back here in years. Last time was with Jimmy Holdrin." She grinned.

"I don't want to hear about it."

"Well, then," Mia said, "we'd better get on with this or we'll freeze our behinds off."

Janice clapped her gloved hands together. "Okay. You're right. No lectures. No sermons. This is all I want to say: I think I understand how you feel. I grew up without a father too. That's what you know, what I've told you: that my parents were divorced when I was seven and I was raised by my mother." She hesitated, exhaled audibly, and looked into Mia's eyes. "What I never told you, Mia, because I was ashamed, was that there never was a divorce. My father just abandoned us and ran off to California. I mean, we didn't know then that he went to California, at least I didn't. I never did find out how much my mother knew."

"That's no big thing," Mia said. "That they didn't get officially divorced. That's what you're ashamed of?"

Janice hugged herself. "Not really. That's not what hurts so much. I even found out, years later—are you ready for a shocker?"

Mia nodded eagerly.

"He got married again and started another family. I found out by accident, but I've got a half sister and a half brother somewhere. We've even got the same last names."

"Wow," Mia said. "He was a bigamist."

"You think you understand now." Janice's voice seemed suddenly tight. It wavered a little.

"About the bigamy."

"No. I don't give a damn about the bigamy. It's the being abandoned . . ." She couldn't finish.

Mia leaned against her mother and then pulled her by the arm. "Come on, let's keep walking." She led her mother along a narrow path off the circular clearing. It was only wide enough for one at a time, and as she walked, she held onto her mother's hand behind her. The path opened onto another clearing, almost exactly like the first—but in the center of it lay a large wooden construction of some sort. It looked like a huge wooden picture frame lying flat with dirty sheets stretched across it and fastened to the wood frame with nails and tacks. Covering most of the sheets were what looked to be bits and pieces of an old rug. The longer she looked the more things Mia saw covering the frame: blankets, old clothes, fragments of fabric . . . "I wonder what that is?" Mia turned and saw that her mother was staring up at the tree tops.

"Listen," Janice said. "Let's finish up this business, okay?" She put her hands on Mia's shoulders. "The reason I started talking about my family is because I wanted to explain something. My mother never stopped loving my father. I swear to you, Mia, up until that woman died, she believed he'd be coming back. I believe it was because, in her heart, she could never deal with the fact that he left her. Now, listen, I don't want to argue about this now, but I think maybe that's how you feel too. Maybe that's why you want to go and live with your father."

"But, Mom—"

"Just let me finish. All I want you to do is think about that. About maybe you feeling abandoned because he left you. All I want you to do is think about the real reasons you want to go live with him. Think about it for a week, maybe two, and then I promise, I swear, I'll talk to you about it with an open mind."

Mia turned away from her mother's touch. "Okay. But it's only one damn summer, I think you're being unreasonable— he *is* my father—and it's not going to make any difference."

Janice was quiet for awhile, and then she said softly, "But you will think about it."

Mia nodded and tried to walk quickly past her mother, but Janice took her by the arm and pulled her close. She embraced her daughter and said, "Now come on. Let's quit fighting."

Mia pulled away. "You always do this. You always make me do things your way."

"That's not true," Janice said, and she stepped close to Mia and put her arms around her. "Look. I promise to be a good girl and discuss things with you reasonably in a week. Okay?"

Mia wiped away tears. "Okay, okay."

"Good." She pointed at the frame. "What *is* that thing."

Together, Mia and Janice walked over to it. When Mia stepped on the sheet, the fabric gave way and she fell through the frame into a hole as deep as she was tall.

"Mia!" Janice yelled. She fell on her knees alongside the frame and looked down only to see Mia looking back up at her. She could have kissed her on the forehead.

"Did you see that?" Mia was standing on a pile of beer cans.

"Who would do such a thing?"

"It's a clubhouse." Mia kicked away a few cans.

"You're lucky you didn't break your neck." The sheet had torn away from the frame in a neat triangle, and now the daylight shone down onto a patch of dirt littered with the same kind of trash that was strewn about the clearing. Where it hung down, the torn sheet formed a kind of tent wall that hid the rest of the clubhouse from view. "What's that?" Janice pointed at Mia's feet, where what looked like it might be a cat's tail stuck out from under the flap of sheet.

Mia kicked the sheet back, revealing the back half of a cat, and, a few feet away, at a right angle to the back half, the front half. Alongside them, the charred body of a kitten stuck up out of the mud. It took Mia a few seconds to realize what she was seeing; then she turned and tried to climb out of the hole, and screamed when she slipped and fell onto her hands and knees.

Janice dropped onto her stomach. She caught Mia under the arm and pulled her out in a single, swift motion.

Mia grimaced and wiped her hands on her jeans. "Damn," she said. "Did you see that?"

Janice picked up the frame and was able to stand it on end and then flip it over, leaving the gaping hole that was under it exposed to the daylight.

"God damn," Mia said. There was still another dead cat at the far end of the hole, and in the center of the pit, side by side, were a muddy pair of white, frilly panties, and maroon briefs.

Several pale yellow condoms were strewn among the beer cans and cigarette butts.

"That's so disgusting," Mia said.

Janice looked into the hole for only a brief moment, and then stepped back and glared at Mia. "Is this the kind of thing they do in these clubs? Torture cats, and . . ." She pointed at the underwear.

"How would I know?" Mia shouted.

"I'm . . . I'll . . ." Janice shook her head. Softly, she said, "I'm going to have to talk to the police about this." Without looking back at Mia, she left the clearing.

Mia looked for another second at the mess on the floor of the pit and then followed her mother.

★   ★

Twenty minutes after the water stopped running in the master bedroom's shower, Janice came into the kitchen looking neat and ministerial in a matching skirt and jacket.

Mia was at the kitchen table flipping through a copy of *Vogue* and sipping hot chocolate from a mug. She was wearing a fluffy, white robe. Her red, pistol-shaped hair dryer was plugged into the wall outlet over the table. "Did I leave you enough hot water?"

"Yes," Janice said. "Thanks for remembering."

Mia nodded and then they both looked at each other until she pointed at the clock. "Better get going."

"Why don't you come?"

"Look at me." She pointed at her robe.

"You could be ready in two minutes. I know you."

"Come on, Mom. You know I don't like going to services."

Janice picked her purse up off the counter and held it firmly under her arm. "I can't change my whole life so that I can get more time to spend with you. But you *could* spend more time with me. You know what I mean? Instead of complaining that I'm never around, why don't you come with me on Sundays? I'd like you to hear my talks. Afterwards, we could have lunch together. It would be nice."

Mia was looking at the floor.

"Okay," Janice muttered. "Fine. It's your life." She threw on her coat and closed the front door behind her with a sharp click.

Mia listened as Janice's car pulled out of the driveway, and when the sound of the engine disappeared, she carried the wireless phone to the kitchen table and dialed her father's number. It rang once and she hung up. She placed the receiver back on its cradle softly and walked into the living room where she fell back onto a plush, blue sofa. From under the coffee table, where she had left it the night before, she took the long, thick, white-and-blue afghan her mother had knitted for her years ago and pulled it up over her shoulders. Then she lay down, cuddled up under the blanket, and flipped on the television using the thin remote-control box, which had been under the couch, also where she had left it the night before. Across the room, the television screen flared and then filled up with the image of three men sitting around a circular table. Mia listened for a few minutes while they talked very reasonably about the oil crisis. Then she turned off the set.

For a while she lay quietly on the couch, looking out the sliding-glass doors off the living room. It had started to snow, and big white flakes were drifting silently to the ground. She went back into the kitchen and hit the redial button on the phone. It rang four times before there was a click and her dad's voice came across the line: "Hi! I'm not here. Ha, ha, ha. If you're a bill collector, tell me how much I owe you, and then forget about ever seeing it. Ha, ha. Just kidding, friends. Leave your name at the beep and I'll catch you later."

Mia frowned and shook her head. After the electronic beep, she said "Dad, you're such a jerk. I want to talk to you. Please call me back. Thanks." She put the receiver down and picked up the phone and her copy of *Vogue,* and carried them into her mother's bedroom, where she slid under the thick, baby-blue comforter on her mother's bed, propped up two down pillows, and started breezing through the pages. When she finished looking at the pictures, she tossed the book to the foot of the bed. Mia liked her mother's bed for its thick mattress. The whole room, however, was a drag. There was a thick bible open—always—on the night table. Over the bed was a big wooden crucifix, and there were several little statues of Christ and Mary spread around the room. Janice had been raised a Roman Catholic, and Mia was convinced that she had become a Unitarian minister only because the Catholics didn't allow women clergy.

She turned on her side and snuggled into the pillows, pulling the quilt tight around her shoulders. She lay quietly for a long while before she got up and looked out the window. Snow was still falling, covering the old, dirty crust with a clean white layer. She stood at the window and watched it accumulate on the ground and in the trees and bushes. Then she got dressed and put on her heavy coat and went out.

The air had turned crisper and colder than it had been when she was out earlier with Janice; and the new-fallen snow freshened the ground and the trees. It was as if someone had taken a broom to the world and swept all the grime away. Mia followed the same path she had taken with Janice. Already the snow had covered up the mud and the footprints and the litter. When she reached the clearing with the clubhouse, she knelt at the edge of the hole and looked down. The cats were gone, as were the condoms and the underwear and all the beer cans. The only thing left at the bottom of the hole was dirt.

Mia stepped back, frightened, and when she looked up she saw a young man across the clearing crouched at the foot of a tree. A rush of fear pushed through her, and for a second she considered running. She took a step away from him, toward where the trees opened on the path out of the woods. When he didn't move, she stopped. His face was boyish and handsome, and he had a look of concern in his eyes, as if he were worried. She asked, "Who are you?"

He answered by repeating her question. "Who are you?"

"My name's Mia. I live around here." She looked him over closely now. He was dressed like a teenager in jeans and sneakers and a light blue ski coat, but she could tell he was older, though not that much older. She guessed early twenties. "Where'd you come from?" she asked. "How come I didn't see you?"

"I don't know," he said. "Maybe you weren't looking. Maybe

I'm the devil. Maybe I just appeared here. You believe in the devil?"

Mia was watching his eyes now: they were blue, a piercing blue. The more she looked at him, the more handsome she found him.

"Lots of kids do, you know. It's like a regular thing, these days." He stood, put his hands in his pockets and walked to the edge of the ditch, directly across from her. He brushed the snow away and sat down, dangling his legs into the hole. "They sacrifice animals to him," he said softly. "They have sexual rituals in his honor. Sometimes they even kill for him. People. Other human beings."

Mia looked at him, and then she looked back to the tree where she had first seen him crouching. Alongside it several stuffed, white plastic garbage bags lay scattered. She said, "You're a cop, aren't you?" She sat across from him on the edge of the ditch.

"You're trusting," he said. "How do you know I'm not about to rape you? How do you know you're not in big trouble out here?"

"Rapists don't clean up the woods. You're taking all that stuff in as evidence, right? You're a cop. You're definitely a cop."

The young man looked at Mia solemnly. "How old are you?"

"Twenty."

"Tell me this, Mia: why would a cop want to take anything out of here for evidence?"

"Because of the cats . . . and the other stuff."

"What cats? What other stuff?"

Mia sighed. "I was here earlier with my mother. I saw," she gestured to the ditch, "what was in there. My mother was probably the one who called you."

The young man nodded and clasped his hands in his lap. He looked down into the ditch and an expression of disgust came over him, a look bordering on fear, as if he were remembering what had been in there. Then he looked at Mia. "And how do you know, Mia, that I'm not the guy who cut up those cats? How do you know I'm not the guy who used those condoms? How do you know that underwear didn't come off a girl I raped?" He was staring now. "How do you know, Mia?"

Mia returned his stare, and the more she looked at him, the younger he seemed, until she felt as though she were looking at a child sitting alone in the middle of a snowy woods. "You're not sure about me, are you? You think I might have something to do with this stuff. You think I might be one of these cult kids or something, don't you?"

"I don't know," he said. "Are you? Are you a cultist? A Satanist?"

"No," Mia said. "And you're not a rapist or a murderer . . . or the devil."

"How do you know that?" he said. "How can you be sure?"

"I know," Mia said. "I just know." She lowered herself into the ditch and looked up at him. "This stuff really scares you, doesn't it? I mean, you're a cop, but you're really scared by this stuff. I can tell."

"Cops can't get scared? If I'm a cop."

Mia crouched down, her back against the rough dirt. When she looked up, she saw his eyes fall from her face to her breasts and then down to her thighs and legs. "Why don't you come down in here," she said. "It's warmer."

From the top of the ditch, the young man looked at her for a long moment, hard, as if he were trying to see something inside her. Then he lowered himself carefully into the hole.

For several seconds they stood facing each other, snow falling over them in the quiet woods. Then Mia said, "Let's do something crazy. Let's not be ourselves."

"Really?" The young man raised his eyebrows as if he were amazed. "And who are we?"

Mia smiled and shrugged. She pointed behind him. "Pull the top over. Let's find out."

He hesitated briefly; then turned and leapt up and pulled the top over the hole. In the dim light, he crouched down in front of her. "Now what? Now what are we two strangers going to do?"

"Come here," she said. She sat down and opened her legs so that he could kneel close to her. When he didn't move, she touched his jacket. "I know this is crazy," she said. "I know this is wild." She ran her hand along his shoulder and down his arm.

He crouched in front of her, quiet, for a long time, just

looking. Then he leaned toward her, as if he wasn't sure what he was going to do next, and he kissed her neck, and then her lips. When he slid his hand under her coat to her stomach, she put her hand over his and lifted it to her breast. He backed away from her, and even in the dim light Mia could see the questioning in his look.

"You are," he said. "You are one of them, aren't you?"

"I'm not," Mia said. "I swear." She moved closer to him. "Trust me," she said, and put his hands on her breasts, and reached under his coat to feel the muscles of his chest and back, and when he lowered his lips to her collar and undid her blouse and her bra to take her breast in his mouth, she held his head in her arms and whispered, "Yes, do that," and held him tightly to her. As she lowered her head and kissed the young man on his temple, she thought for a moment about Janice, who would be up in the pulpit now, preaching her sermon, winging it on the notes she had managed. Then the thought disappeared and she closed her eyes and listened to the quiet of snow falling in the woods, concentrating on the feel of his lips and his hands as they moved slowly over her body.

SOMETHING NEW, SOMETHING DIFFERENT

Jimmy's reflection lurched in the window glass as the subway car bounced and swayed. Eleven years old and already in eighth grade, he was returning to Williamsburg from a trip to Manhattan. His friend Warren, who was fourteen and lived down the block from him, and who had suggested they cut school to see a porno movie, sat alongside him in the subway car reading a book titled *My Life with Incest*, the cover of which he had torn off and replaced with the cover from a condensed version of *The Idiot*.

"Oh, man!" Warren whispered, nudging Jimmy. "His own sister, man. Can you believe it?"

Jimmy turned away from the window and slid down in his seat. "After what we just saw, I believe anything."

"What? What are you talking?"

"What am I talking? Warren, there were eight people in

one bed, all . . . connected." Jimmy made a view frame with his hands and moved and turned it to different angles, as if he were a director arranging a shot. "I still can't figure out what they were all doing even though I was watching them do it. You know what I mean?"

Warren squinted at him. "You're a weird kid, Jimmy. You know that? You're definitely weird."

"Look who's talking."

"I shouldn't have taken you," Warren said. "You're too young."

"I cut school same as you."

"So what were you doing, Brain? Thinking about calculus or something?"

Jimmy crossed his eyes and stuck out his tongue, which never failed to make Warren laugh. "You really want to know what I was thinking about?"

"Yeah. No. Didn't I just ask?"

"You promise not to laugh?"

"I won't laugh." Warren put his hand over his mouth, as if he couldn't hold back the giggles. Then he said, "I'm only kidding, man. Go ahead. Tell me."

Jimmy hesitated because Warren was the only kid in homeroom who didn't treat him as though he were some kind of freak for getting skipped two grades. He didn't want to say anything that might make him change his mind. But if he couldn't tell a friend, what good was having one? "You know what I was thinking about?" He lowered his voice to a whisper as the train stopped at the Bushwick Avenue station and one of the other three passengers got off. Then as it took off again and the roar filled the car, he spoke up. "I was thinking about the people up there doing it. I was, like, wondering who they were. You know what I mean? They have to be somebody, right? You know?"

"They're actors."

"Sure, but I mean, they're really doing it. They're not acting. I mean, what if they have a kid someday and he sees it or something?"

"Get out of here," Warren said. "That's really what you were thinking?"

Jimmy was embarrassed. "Yeah," he said. "I can't help it. I been thinking a lot about that kind of stuff lately."

Warren shook his head and stretched out in his seat. He was a full two inches taller than Jimmy. Dressed in boots, blue jeans, and a red T-shirt, with his hair slicked back on the sides and arranged so that a neat curlicue pointed down over his forehead to the bridge of his nose, he looked meaner, tougher, and older than he was—especially alongside a kid like Jimmy whose short hair was parted on the side and combed neatly across his head, and who wasn't even allowed to wear blue jeans to school, let alone a T-shirt. "I bet you never even seen a real girl naked," he said.

Jimmy turned to look out the window as another station flashed by. He said, "We're the next stop." Then he asked, "Have you?"

Warren shook his head. He picked up his book and held it to his chest. "Man," he said, "if I had a sister, I'd do it to her all the time."

"You would not," Jimmy said. "You're such a jerk. If you had a sister, you wouldn't even think about her like that. You wouldn't even like anybody else thinking about her like that."

"Yeah?" Warren seemed interested. "How come? How come it's different if she's your sister?"

"Because," Jimmy said. "I don't know. It's like it's different then, that's all."

"Oh." Warren frowned and sank down in his seat, as if he were suddenly very sad.

Jimmy wished Warren would finish the dumb book he was reading so that he'd quit talking about sisters the way he was. He didn't understand anything. Jimmy's sister Annie was his favorite person in the world. She was twenty-one and married and lived upstairs from him in the second-floor apartment. Jimmy spent more time upstairs with Annie and Joey, her husband, than he did downstairs with his parents. A long time ago, before he was born, when Annie was only nine years old, she had been attacked by a man in the alley right outside their house. Jimmy had only found out about this a few months ago. He had been up in Annie's apartment during the day, when Annie and Joey were both out working, and he had noticed her diary on the floor by her bed. It was one of those books with a strap and a lock on it, so that no one could read it without the key. Jimmy had often seen the diary left out, but what caught his attention this time was a yellowing strip of newspaper sticking out like a bookmark. He thought about it for only a second; then he stuck in another sheet of paper to mark the place and pulled out the newspaper.

The story was about Annie, about how she had been "attacked" in the alley and "left to die." This was hard for Jimmy to believe—that something like this could have happened in his family, and no one had even said a word to him about it. Half of him didn't really believe it at all until he came to the part that said she had been stabbed twice in the back, and then he knew it was true and the terribleness of it sliced into him and made him feel sick and sweaty. He sat on the bed telling himself that it had happened a long time ago and that Annie was okay now. He repeated that to himself again and again before putting the article back in the diary and going outside to play; but he avoided Annie that night and for a few nights after, because he was afraid if he saw her he'd blurt out what he knew.

This thing about Annie was Jimmy's deepest secret, something he hadn't talked about to anyone. No one knew that he knew; and if he told anyone, he'd have to admit to looking at the article in Annie's diary. If Annie found out, she'd be disappointed in him. And how he knew for sure that she had been stabbed—that was also mixed up with the secret. One night last summer just before dark, he had been playing ball by himself out in the backyard, and he had hit a pink rubber Spaldene up onto Mr. Tarini's roof. Mr. Tarini was an old guy with a huge pot belly who kept a loaded air pistol by the back window so that he could shoot any kid who tried to climb the fire escape up to his roof. Jimmy had dodged Mr. Tarini's BBs once in the past and he didn't want to try it again. He had about given up on the ball when an idea came to him.

He went inside, looked up Mr. Tarini's phone number, and called him. He had intended to tell him there was a package for him sitting on the stoop outside his door; but when no one answered, that made things even simpler. He climbed up onto the roof, retrieved the ball, and was about to start climbing down when he saw Annie.

It was almost dark out, and the bright yellow light through a pair of oversized windows made the details of Annie's room crisp and clear. The windows were only twenty feet away, and Jimmy was looking down into the bedroom, over the top of a pair of café curtains, at Annie. She was wearing her blue terry cloth robe as she bent over and rummaged through her dresser. Jimmy called her name and waved to her, and when she stood up and turned to face the window, he thought she had heard him. He smiled and waved again, but then Annie threw something white and flimsy onto the bed and in a single motion shrugged off the blue robe and let it fall to the floor.

It took Jimmy a second to realize that Annie didn't know he was watching her, and then another second to realize she was standing in his sight fully naked. He stepped backward toward the fire escape and looked away, but then he stopped and turned to look again. This time he caught sight of her as she stood closer to the window, still undressed, with her back toward him. Then she walked out of the bedroom. Now those two pictures of Annie without clothes—standing facing him by the bed and with her back to him by the window—were framed in Jimmy's mind as real and clear and hard-edged as photographs. It was when she was close to the window that he saw the two oblong scars, one a little higher than the other, a couple of inches apart, in the middle of her back. He had been curious about them ever since. Until he found the newspaper article.

When they reached their stop, Warren and Jimmy raced each other out of the station and up the stairs into the bright daylight. There were only a few more days of school remaining before summer vacation and it was already hot out on the street.

Jimmy said to Warren, "I just remembered. I did see a real girl naked once."

"Bullshit," Warren said. "Who?"

"My sister."

"Annie? You saw Annie naked? When? Wait a minute: was this when she was a baby or something, man?"

"Don't be dumb, Warren. I wasn't even alive when Annie was a baby. She's eleven years older than me."

"Oh. Yeah." Warren stuck his hands in his pockets. "I don't believe you anyway. What'd she look like?"

"I'm not telling you."

"You're lying."

"I am not."

"Okay." Warren stopped and seemed to ponder matters for a minute. "Okay," he repeated. "You don't have to tell me what she looked like; just tell me what you saw."

"What do you mean?"

"Like did you see the front or the back? Everything? Just part?"

"Everything."

"Get out of here!" Warren yelled.

"I did!"

"You did not. What'd you do? Peek at her?"

"No," Jimmy said. "It was an accident."

"Yeah, man. You walked in on her in the shower and she turned around so you could see everything."

"Shut up, Warren."

"Well?"

"I was up on Tarini's roof getting my ball back that I'd hit up there and you can see down into Annie's bedroom from there, and when I looked I saw her get undressed. She must have been going to take a shower."

"And you watched?"

"It was only a second or two. I didn't really. You'd better not tell anybody."

"I'm not going to tell. You really saw Annie naked. Man. What'd she do, forget to close the curtains?"

Jimmy shook his head. They were only a few doors away from his house. "She's got those curtains that only cover the bottom half of the window. You can see over them from up on Tarini's roof." As soon as Jimmy said this, he wished he hadn't.

Warren was silent.

In front of his house, Jimmy said, "Warren, you'd better not be thinking what I think you're thinking."

Warren grinned. "I ain't thinking nothing, man."

"Warren!" Jimmy said. "You'd better not!"

94

Warren shook his head, still grinning, and trotted away. "Warren!" Jimmy yelled after him. "Warren!"

⋆   ⋆

"What do you keep looking out that window?" Jimmy's mother stood in the doorway between the kitchen and the living room with her hands on her hips. She was a short, heavy woman who wore a wig of red hair styled in a bouffant to please her husband. "Well?"

Jimmy sat in an overstuffed chair by the living room window. His father was stretched out on the sofa in his undershirt watching the Perry Como show. Jimmy had been watching, with only mild interest, a man in a tuxedo juggling butcher knives. Every few minutes he turned around to look out the window and across the yard to Mr. Tarini's fire escape. "I don't know," he said. "I thought I heard something."

His mother pointed at him. "I'm making you a glass of milk and honey. It's good for the nerves."

His father shot up on the couch. "He's eleven years old, for God's sake! He doesn't have any nerves!" He accented each word with a bobbing right hand, the ball of his thumb gently nestled in the center of the other four outstretched fingers.

"Now you're going to tell me how to raise my children?"

"Mom," Jimmy said. "I don't want a glass—"

His father turned sharply. "Do what your mother says!" He gestured to his wife. "Go ahead. Make it for him." Then, when she left the room, he turned back to Jimmy. "Quit looking out the window or I'll break your neck."

Jimmy fell back in his chair, but a minute later, while his dad was engrossed in watching a woman in sequined tights cross a narrow wire on a bicycle, he got up and knelt by his head. "Can I go up to see Annie, Dad?"

"Go ahead," his father said. When Jimmy crossed in front of the couch, his dad reached out and pinched his leg.

Jimmy jumped and ran into the kitchen, where his mother was stirring honey into a glass of warm milk. "I'm going up to Annie's," he said as he took the milk from her. "Dad said okay."

"A half hour, you have to be in bed." His mother put a hand behind his head and kissed him on the cheek before she started for the living room to join her husband. "Knock before you go in and don't be a scucc'."

Jimmy carried the glass of warm milk up the first flight of stairs past his bedroom and up the second flight to Annie's apartment. He knocked on the door once and walked in. Annie was in the living room ironing a dress and watching Perry Como. She was wearing a pink muumuu that looked like it should belong to his mother. It flopped around her small body like a tent as she worked at the ironing board; and still, somehow, probably because of her smooth, dark skin and her neatly brushed hair, when she nodded to acknowledge Jimmy she looked young and pretty. She looked like a teenager playing at being a housewife.

Jimmy said, "Where's Joey?"

Annie gestured toward the kitchen, where Joey spent a lot of time reading. He was going to night school in the city. He wanted to be an architect.

Jimmy finished off the milk and honey in three swallows and put the empty glass down on top of the TV. "Mom made it for my nerves." He took a seat on the floor by a yellow plastic laundry basket.

Annie looked down at him. "What nerves? You have a problem?" She turned off the iron, picked up the laundry basket and carried it into the bedroom. Jimmy followed her in and watched as she went about putting the ironed clothes away. He sat on the bed and looked up, over the top of the café curtains, out onto Mr. Tarini's roof.

After Annie put the last of the clothes away, she sat on the bed next to Jimmy. "What are you talking about, 'nerves'?"

"You know Mom." He lay back on the bed and pointed out the window. "Hey. Look at that. You can see Mr. Tarini's roof from here."

Annie looked to the window and then back to Jimmy. She had straight, shoulder-length brown hair that she was always pushing back behind her ears. "So what?"

Jimmy went to the window. "Nothing. But did you ever notice before?"

Annie gave him a searching look. "Do you want to talk about something?"

96

Jimmy shook his head.

Annie seemed tired and a little annoyed. She pointed to the bedroom door. "I'm taking a shower."

"A shower? Why? That's bad for your skin."

"A shower is bad for your skin?"

"Yeah. I read about it."

Annie stared at him. Finally, she said, "You want to get out of here, Jimmy? I'll risk taking a shower."

"You really shouldn't, Annie." Jimmy stayed put, planted by the window.

Annie pushed her hair behind her ears. "What's with you tonight?"

Jimmy shrugged.

"You don't want to talk?"

"Uh uh."

"Well, then" . . . She pointed to the door again, her voice getting louder. "Go."

"Well, really, Annie . . . He sat down on the bed next to her and curled his legs under him. "I did want to talk."

She gestured for him to go ahead.

Jimmy thought for a second, and then, to his own surprise, he said, "Can I tell you something I did bad?"

Annie nodded, interested now.

He lowered his voice. "I cut school today and went to see one of those dirty movies in the city."

"Where in the city?"

"Forty-second Street."

"Forty-second Street!" She looked at Jimmy as if he had to be crazy to go there, as if she could hardly believe what he had said. "That's dangerous. Did anything happen to you?"

He shook his head.

"You sure?"

"Nothing happened."

"You know you could tell me. You know I'd understand and it'd be just between us."

"I swear," Jimmy said. "Nothing happened except the movie."

Annie folded her arms under her breasts. "Okay," she said. "So, what, now you feel guilty because of what you saw?"

"Not guilty, weird."

"You mean, like confused? Like you can't understand what you saw?"

"I understand. It just makes me feel weird."

Annie took a deep breath and let it out slowly in a long sigh. "Look, Jimmy," she said, her face darker, "if you want to know stuff about sex, I'll get Joey to talk to you, okay? I think man-to-man would be better, don't you?"

Jimmy shrugged.

"But promise me you're not going back to Forty-second Street. There are sick people there, Jimmy. You have to take my word on that. Some of the sickest people in the world go to places like that. You understand?"

Jimmy nodded, and then, to his surprise, his eyes filled with tears. "Annie," he said. "I'd never let anyone—" Then suddenly he was hugging his sister and crying, everything confused. He meant, he thought, that he was sorry about what happened to her when she was a little girl—but that got mixed up with looking in her diary, and seeing her from the roof, until it was all a jumble and he was just crying.

As if Jimmy somehow couldn't hear her, Annie whispered to Joey, who had sat down on the bed beside her, "He went to a sex movie in the city and it's got him all messed up."

Joey stared down at a thick textbook he was holding firmly by the edges and pressing hard against, as if he were trying to crumple it—an isometric exercise. The muscles of his chest and arms bulged and pushed at the fabric of his short-sleeved shirt. He put the book down. "Jimmy," he said. "Do you want to come in the other room with me and we can talk about it? About the movie?"

Jimmy was looking away from Annie and Joey, down at the bed, trying to think of what to say, when, from out in the backyard he heard the muffled "pop! pop!" of Mr. Tarini's air pistol, followed by the clatter of the fire escape and more pops and then Mr. Tarini shouting in Italian. Jimmy jumped to the window in time to see a pair of legs fall over Mr. Tarini's fence and disappear.

"What the hell was that?" Joey threw the window open and looked out. Annie and Jimmy squeezed themselves together and leaned out with him.

"Mr. Tarini!" Joey yelled. "Everything okay?"

"I miss him!" Mr. Tarini yelled back. "I miss the little thief!" Then he strung a line of Italian curses together and slammed the window shut.

Annie squeezed out from between her husband and her brother and sat back down on the bed. "This neighborhood gets worse all the time."

Joey closed the window. He put his hand on Jimmy's shoulder. "I got an idea. Let's all go in the kitchen and have a snack. I'm starving."

Jimmy shook his head. "No thanks. I'd better get to bed. It's getting late."

Joey said, "Are you sure?"

Annie added, "Wouldn't you feel better if we talked a little more?"

"No, honest," Jimmy said. "All of a sudden, I feel much better. Honestly. I think I was just tired or something. Really. I feel a lot better now."

Annie said, "Probably did you good to let it all out. You sure you're okay?"

"Really." He kissed her on the cheek. "Good night. I'll see you tomorrow."

"Okay. And no more dangerous stuff. You promise?"

"I promise."

Jimmy started to leave the room and Joey followed him. In the hallway, they sat down together on the top of the stairs.

Joey said, "Listen, Jimmy. I know you can't talk to your parents about sex, so I want you to know, if you have any questions, you can ask me. It'll be private that way, okay?"

"Thanks," Jimmy said. "But I think I already know everything about sex. It's just the movie made me feel weird, that's all."

"What do you mean by weird?"

Jimmy turned so that he was facing Joey. "I keep thinking about those people in the movie. I imagine them sitting around the dinner table with their family, you know, and they have regular clothes on and stuff. I mean, they probably have brothers and sisters and everything, right? So, I keep wondering about them as regular people."

Joey held his chin in his hand. He was quiet for a long

while. Then he said, "So what's the problem. I don't get it."

"Me neither. But I think about their kids seeing the movie, or their mothers and fathers or something, and then it's almost like I feel like I was getting caught doing it." He shook his head.

Joey said, "You're a lot smarter than most people, so, I think, maybe you see things a little differently. I don't know. Maybe you feel bad for them because it's such a sad job. After all, they're really just prostitutes, and being a prostitute's got to be one of the saddest things in the world."

"But it's not like I'm a prostitute or anything. How come I feel like I'm getting caught?"

"Well, you did give them your money, right? I mean, in a sense, you're paying them to do it, right?"

"I don't think so. I mean, they would have done it anyway. It didn't matter if I paid or not."

"Well, look," Joey said. "You're not going to Forty-second Street again, right? You promised your sister."

"I won't," Jimmy said. "Don't worry."

Joey put his arm around Jimmy's shoulder, pulled him close for a second, and then released him. "Just remember what I said." Then he went in, closing and bolting the door behind him.

Jimmy walked slowly down the stairs and through the hallway to his bedroom, where he sat on the edge of his bed and undressed slowly, pulling off one piece of clothing at a time and then resting. When he was down to his underwear, he got up and looked at himself in the full-length mirror attached to the back of his closet door. He wondered if he'd ever have muscles like Warren, or maybe even like Joey. He lifted his arms and flexed and then shook his head. He took off his undershirt and underpants and looked at himself naked in the mirror. His penis was a skinny, pinkish thing—nothing like the men in the movie. He tucked it down between his legs. Now he looked like what a lot of the girls his age must look like: just a smooth place there, a gently curving surface. Was this what it felt like to be a girl? He touched his breasts. He squinted his eyes, trying to see himself as if he were a girl. Then he opened his legs and let his sex pop back into place, turning himself into a boy again. Were girls like this, he wondered? Did girls look in the mirror and wonder what it's like to be a boy?

Tired, he closed the closet door and got into his pajamas. In bed, he made a circle with his arms and he tried to imagine he was holding another person, a girl. He leaned into the circle and moved his hips, the way the men in the movie had moved their hips over the women they held. He closed his eyes and tried to imagine that there really was a girl inside the circle and he leaned into her hard, and stayed that way a long time, until he was close to asleep and half-dreaming—half-thinking, until it was as if he and the girl were the same thing, and there was nothing but the one thing the two of them made together, and he felt, strangely, as if he were something different, a ball or a circle soaring into something new. Then his arms fell to his sides, startling him awake. In the dark, he lay very still and tried not to let any thoughts into his mind, the way he always did when he didn't want to wake up, when he really wanted a dream to continue.

But a picture from the porno movie came to mind anyway. Several men and women were all naked on the floor. Their bodies made a writhing circle as each one chewed on the sex of the next one, and he could hear again the strange loud moans and groans that filled the dark, smelly theater. Something about that particular scene in the movie, the circle of bodies, each segment a person biting and being bitten, made him feel odd—as if he were somehow off balance. He sat up in bed to try to shake the sounds and pictures, but then he found himself thinking about the two oblong scars, the pale white marks hidden between Annie's shoulder blades and that was even worse. Finally, he got out of bed and walked through the dark to make sure the bedroom door was locked. Then he checked the windows, and satisfied that they too were locked, he got back in bed and pressed his head into the pillow. He tried hard to think about that first dream—when he had put his arms around an imaginary girl and leaned into her and they became one thing, a circle moving together through the dark. For a long time, he lay in bed quietly, thinking hard, concentrating, trying by force of will to make himself dream the dream he wanted.

THE
GIRL
AT THE
WINDOW

———————

It was still dark when he awoke, his eyes opening as suddenly as if he hadn't been asleep at all. This morning it was something other than the baby fussing or a frightening dream that woke him. This morning it was his wife, though it took him a minute to realize. She was running in her sleep, the way a puppy will, her feet shuffling over the sheets with a jerky, kicking motion.

When she stopped, Chris sat up in bed. He scratched the back of his neck against the ornate wicker headboard May had picked out when they were first married. He was tall and he had been skinny all his life, but this morning as he looked down at his bare chest, at the line of his ribs and the taut skin of his stomach, he thought he looked especially fragile. He was having a hard time eating lately. He had been having trouble with his nerves for months, and when he was nervous he didn't eat well—but it was too early in the day to start worrying. He looked down at his wife just as her body twitched, as if jumping away from something, and he thought of how, as a child, she would run in circles, making hysterical, inarticulate noises and shaking her hands frantically. She did this when witnessing something especially violent, which happened often in her home, since her parents were alcoholics. When she first told him this, years ago—she was already thirty then and remembering things she had seen when seven and eight— the memory was still so strong she couldn't keep from crying. Her mood had been good, and in the middle of a sentence describing how she would shake her hands as she ran, the crying burst out of her, suddenly, as if it punched its way through some inner wall and leapt out uncontrolled, changing her mood in an instant so that for a while she cried hard against his chest, and then sobbed for a long time after. Chris had cried with her, hurt by that picture of May so defenseless, injured. Usually, when that image came to mind he wanted to do something nice for her—bring home ice cream or take her out to dinner—but this morning it made him think of the girl who lived in the second-story apartment of the house next door, the girl who watched him every morning as he left for work.

She was a pretty girl, an exceptionally pretty girl. Chris and May guessed her age at five or six. She had big, brown eyes and auburn hair, and a full, round face with plump cheeks. Once, when Chris saw part of an old Shirley Temple movie, he thought of the girl at the window, she looked so much like the child actress. But this real child's life wouldn't make a script for a Shirley Temple movie. Her mother, and her mother's current boyfriend—the fourth or fifth man Chris had seen around the house in the past four years— were both drunks, and the child was abused. She seemed always to have a fresh cut or bruise. May had called all the social service agencies. At each one she got the same response: the case was being looked into by Child Welfare. Eventually she gave up, knowing firsthand how little the authorities can help. Once Chris tried calling, after the girl showed up at the window with two black eyes, a cut bottom lip, and the right side of her face swollen. At first he just looked away, but when he looked up again she tried to smile at him, as she usually did, and then cringed at the pain. Chris turned around, went back upstairs, and called the same agencies May had called—and got the same answers. At Child Welfare he asked: "Can you at least tell me the girl's name?" "No," a woman answered. "I can't. But," she said, "why don't you just ask her?"

Chris went back to the car, and when the girl came to the window to watch him leave—it was summer and she was standing at an open window—he called up to her. "Hi," he said, trying to sound friendly. "What's your name?"

The girl looked down at him, careful this time not to smile. She didn't answer.

He called to her again. "Won't you tell me your name?" he said. "I'm Chris."

This time the girl began to look troubled. She raised her right hand to her shoulder and waved hesitantly.

Chris stared up at her. As usual, she was carefully dressed and groomed. Her hair was soft and healthy, and she wore a blue-and-white checked dress with a shiny red belt. Everything about her looked neat and well cared for, which only made the injuries to her face stand out more startlingly.

He tried one more time. "Won't you tell me your name?" he asked. "I'm not a bad guy, you know."

The girl looked even more troubled, as if she were about to cry. She backed slowly away from the window until she was out of sight.

Since then Chris had tried not to think about the girl, though she was there every morning watching him as he opened the garage door, backed the car out and closed the door behind him before driving off to work. He couldn't imagine what there was in this ritual to draw the child so faithfully to the window. He imagined she was living through horrors much like the ones his wife suffered as a child. May had seen her house torn up repeatedly by her father. She had seen her brothers and sisters beaten till they lost consciousness. Once her father held her pet cat in front of her and strangled it until its eyes bulged out of its head, and then crushed it against the wall. Once, after he threw her mother out a second-story window, he came looking for May, who was hiding under a bed trying not to breathe. In dreams she still saw him peering under the bed, his arms reaching for her. She remembered that he passed out, and she remembered climbing over his body to look out the window and see her mother throwing up on the lawn below. She remembered, too, her mother chasing her with a knitting needle, and her mother stabbing her father in the cheek with scissors. She remembered her father crawling out the back door, trailing a line of blood.

Chris looked down at May and wondered what, at thirty-six, she was still running from. He reached under the soft beige quilt that fell around his waist and over May's neck, and he touched her back and shoulders. She was drenched, as he half expected, the sheets around her wet where the sweat dropped from her body. This happened often when she was having nightmares. Chris had learned long ago not to wake her when she was like this. If awakened she might remember the dream, which would leave her upset for days or weeks; but if allowed to sleep through the nightmares, she never remembered them. Now Chris was concerned that the alarm would ring in a few minutes and wake her, so he rubbed her neck and shoulder gently, hoping to interrupt her dream.

The muscles of her back were knotted and tight. He pushed back the quilt. May had her knees pulled up to her chin, and her hands stretched out in front of her, so that she looked exactly as though she were crouched in the middle of a complicated dive. He massaged her back and shoulders, running his hand along her spine and down into the soft flesh below, and he felt her back begin to loosen. Then she stretched out her legs, turned on her stomach, and pressed her head against his thigh. Her eyes opened for a moment and she twisted her head to look up at Chris before she nuzzled back down against the pillow. In a few seconds she was once again sleeping soundly. Then it was seven o'clock and the alarm rang.

May dug her head deeper into the pillow. Chris hurried out of bed to keep the sharp buzzing from awakening Lucy, but before he could turn around he heard the familiar sounds she made as she climbed easily over wooden bars and dropped onto a chair that May had placed alongside the crib. When he turned around she was standing in the doorway, her arms open, her blue eyes glittering, and through her smile she said

106

"Daa Eee," as if surprised, slightly shy, and somehow a little embarrassed to find her father. Then she scampered across the bare wood floor and into Chris's arms as he knelt down to pick her up.

May turned on her back and slid over in the bed, giving Chris and the baby room to sit alongside her.

"Give Mommy a hug good morning," Chris said. He knelt on the bed at May's side.

Lucy jumped away from him to wrap her arms around her mother's neck. When she finished squeezing, which lasted a few seconds, she backed up. Holding her mother's chin at arm's length she made sharp, smacking sounds with her lips.

Chris and May laughed.

"You giving Mommy kisses?" May asked.

Lucy looked at May for a long moment, as if trying to think of some response; then shook her body from head to toe and threw herself back on the bed. May squeezed Lucy's belly, which made her laugh hysterically and squirm over on her back, trying to escape.

Chris stepped away. His daughter was wearing a light blue blanket-sleeper that accented the blueness of her eyes and made them shine. Soft strands of her child's blond hair curled over her collar. He wanted to be happy this morning with May and Lucy. He wanted to join them in a few minutes of morning play. But he was beginning already, as had been happening for months now, to feel distanced from what was going on around him—as if somehow he wasn't a part of things, as if he were watching a movie. It was frightening, and when it was at its worst nothing seemed real: voices sounded as though they were coming through a tunnel, and he re-played every word and action in his mind as if narrating a story. He wanted to tell May about it, but he was afraid such weakness would frighten her. Chris had always prided himself on being strong and stable. It was one of the reasons, he was sure, that May loved him. He was afraid of what might happen to the relationship if he were no longer strong. He touched May on the shoulder. "Time to get going," he said. He kissed her on the cheek and started for the shower.

Under the hot water, he bent his head, took a deep breath, and held the air in his lungs for a few seconds before letting it out slowly. He didn't understand what was happening. He and May had been married for seven years—happily. He liked his job. He liked family life. What was it then that was bothering him? What was happening? In his heart he was afraid he was going crazy. There were madmen on the street all around him. The city and the nation were full of them. People cracked all the time, were led off to asylums. Chris saw no reason it couldn't happen to him. And what would happen to Lucy then? And what would happen to May?

His stomach started to feel queasy. "This is crazy," he said. "It's my damn nerves." But he felt, more than anything, as if he wanted to cry. "It's probably just the job," he told himself. "It's pressure." He reasoned that, even though he liked his job, it was a new job, and he must, inwardly, be under more pressure to succeed than he realized.

Chris worked for a corporation that made automobile parts. He was hired, a few months before he married May, as a factory worker at minimum wage. Since then he had gotten promotion after promotion, until, when Lucy was born, he was taken out of the factory and given a job as an administrative assistant. He still didn't earn much money, but some of the corporate officers made forty and fifty thousand, and he knew—if he did well—it was possible he could wind up in a similar position. Chris also knew he was lucky to have found such a job. Before he met May, he had moved around the country working as a laborer. He wanted to do well, and he dreamed of building a house in the country for May and Lucy, and of having a little brother for Lucy if they could ever afford it.

The thought of the house he would someday build calmed Chris a little. He stepped out of the shower, dried himself off, and resolved that it was the pressure of his new position that was bothering him. In time he'd adjust. While May changed and fed Lucy, he dressed and made himself coffee, and in twenty minutes he was at the kitchen door kissing May and Lucy good-bye.

"Are you okay this morning?" May asked as she stepped back from Chris. She was holding the door open with one arm while holding the baby with the other.

"Sure," Chris said. May was wearing one of his red flannel

shirts, and Chris noticed, suddenly, how attractive she looked. Her sandy-blond hair appeared almost brown next to Lucy's, but her eyes were just as bright blue as the baby's. She looked much younger than she was—mid-twenties at the oldest. Knowing what May had been through as a child, Chris was always surprised by her looks: her skin was smooth and fair, and in the clean, straight lines of her eyebrows and the roundness of her lips, and in the way her nose turned just slightly upward, there was an innocence he could never have expected. The hardness, the callousness he would have assumed necessary for her survival just wasn't there. Chris touched her cheek and kissed her once more before starting down the stairs.

Once out the door he waved to the child, who was waiting for him at her window. When he first looked up, she had her nose and lips pressed playfully against the glass, but when she saw him, she backed away quickly, as if embarrassed to be caught acting childishly. She waved back, as she always did, raising her right hand timidly to her shoulder and moving it back and forth hesitantly, as if uncertain of the proper behavior in this situation. It was an endearing wave that always hurt a little, first thing in the morning. As Chris backed the car out of the driveway and onto the road, he felt thankful that at least this morning there wasn't a mark on her. She looked like a normal cute little girl.

On the way to work he thought more about the house he would someday build. For a while after Lucy was born, when the idea of building a house was a passion with him, Chris had subscribed to *Architectural Digest*, and in one issue he had seen a house built in a rural part of New York that had a semicircular living room, the outer wall of which was glass. Beyond the glass wall there was a little clearing surrounded by woods on three sides, and in the center of the clearing there was a wood counter that housed a bird bath, a salt block, and a tray for grain. The owner of the house wrote that birds and animals came there day and night to feed, that deer were common visitors, and among the more exotic creatures he had seen in his clearing were quail, partridge, wild turkey, and a bobcat. One morning he had walked into the living room at first light to find a huge, absolutely white snow owl perched on the bird bath. He only saw it for a second before it unfolded its long wings and flew away, but for that second the whole window was filled with the white light of its moving wings, and for a long time the muffled, windy sound of its flight stayed with him. He called it a vision of perfection.

Chris believed him. He wanted Lucy to grow up seeing such things. He thought about a house in the country, and he imagined a driveway a mile long that twisted and turned through pathless woods. It occurred to him then that this dream was not just a dream—that with hard work such a house in the country could be his, and a second later his eyes filled with tears and he prayed that God would keep him healthy; and though in his mind all he said was healthy, he knew what he meant was emotionally, mentally healthy. In the driver's seat he gritted his teeth and squeezed the steering wheel tightly. The sense of not having any self, of *not being* came over him strongly. A neat line of sweat formed at the top of his forehead as he waited for the fear to pass.

Getting to work helped. He spent most of the morning talking with acquaintances. While he talked and occasionally worked he felt better, though the fear was always there, like a shadow he couldn't see but knew was behind him. Then, during lunch, he was called out of the cafeteria for a phone call. It was May. An ambulance had come to their neighbor's apartment and taken the girl's mother away. No one had told May the details, but she had seen the woman being carried to the ambulance and she knew the boyfriend had beaten her. She didn't need to be told.

"Did they arrest the guy?" Chris asked.

"Come on!" May said. "Who'd press charges?"

"What about the girl?"

"That's why I called," May said. "She's here. I saw her standing by our garage after the ambulance left, so I went down and brought her up. They were going to leave her with that animal."

Chris tried to think. "Okay," he heard himself say. "I'll come home."

May answered: "I think that would be good."

Chris nodded, as if May could see him. "You just keep the door locked," he said. He thought about the few times he had seen the man next door. He was big: six-six, six-seven at the least. He had perfectly square shoulders and liked to wear checked flannel shirts, so that he cut a figure more appropriate to a lumber camp than a city apartment. "You do have the doors locked?" he asked.

"Yes," May said. "Just come home."

Half an hour later, Chris pulled into the driveway. He parked the car, closed the garage door, and looked up at his neighbor's apartment. The window shades were up, but there was no activity inside. He unlocked the door to his building, then carefully locked it behind him before climbing the stairs to his apartment. May was waiting for him at the door. Behind her he could see into the living room where the neighbor's girl was sitting properly on the edge of his rocker with her hands folded in her lap. She was wearing a neatly pressed, leaf-green dress.

"She won't talk," May said.

Chris walked into the kitchen and closed the door behind him. He put his hand on May's shoulder, and as he started to talk Lucy came waddling-running out of her room, her arms jammed with stuffed animals. She was heading for the rocker, but when she saw Chris out of the corner of her eye she stopped and dropped all the toys. Instead of running to Chris, as he expected her to do, she put her hands on her hips and said, "Daa Ee home?"

"Daddy's home," Chris answered. He picked Lucy up and carried her to the rocker. "Well," he said to the girl who was smiling and looking eagerly at him. "I'm finally going to find out what your name is. I've been wondering for a long time."

The girl continued smiling, but now there was a touch of apprehension in her face.

"This is my wife May," Chris said, pointing. "And this is my daughter Lucy." He picked up one of the dozens of toys that were spread around the foot of the chair. Lucy had emptied her toy box for her. "You have apparently already met Lucy!" Chris was trying his best to be amusing.

The girl smiled brightly at his tone of voice but still wouldn't talk.

"And I'm Chris," he said. "You remember me." Then he put Lucy down in the chair beside the girl. She looked surprised for a moment, then happy. Lucy wrapped her arms around the girl's chest and gave her a hug. Chris smiled at the girl. "You entertain Lucy for a while," he said. He went back to the kitchen with May following.

"What do you think?" May asked. She was rubbing the heels of her clasped hands back and forth against each other—something she did only when very nervous.

"Maybe she can't talk," Chris said.

"She can hear," May said. "She came when I called her."

"What do you think we should do?"

"I called Child Welfare. They're sending someone."

Chris put his arm around May, and together they went into the living room and did their best to entertain the children.

Four hours later no one had come for the girl, and Chris had spent the last hour on the phone being transferred from person to person as he tried to contact the right social worker. He had hung up the phone ten minutes ago after being promised someone would call him back in five minutes. The buzzer for the front door rang as he was about to call again. Chris pressed the button for the kitchen intercom and asked who was there. A voice that sounded tired even through the static answered. "Robert Barrows, Child Welfare," it said. Chris let him in and met him on the stairs outside the kitchen. May stayed in the living room with the children.

Barrows was a young man who looked like he needed sleep. Part of his shirt hung over the belt of his trousers, and his sport jacket was wrinkled. There were dark circles under his eyes. He explained, standing at the top of the stairs, that the social worker assigned to the girl's family was on vacation. The agency, though, had contacted her, and after they had explained the situation, she had recommended that the child be returned to the father.

Chris said, "It's not her father! It's some drunk who just beat her mother half to death!"

"But it is her father," Barrows explained. "I just talked to the mother. She'll be out of the hospital in the morning, and she wants her daughter home."

"This animal's her father? I've been here four years and he just showed up a few months ago."

Barrows was silent for a long moment. Then he spoke

softly. "Look," he said. "I shouldn't tell you this, but the mother's the problem. She's an alcoholic, was abused herself, and every man she takes up with beats her, and . . ." He hesitated. He stood there awkwardly and put his hands in his trouser pockets. "That little girl you have with you has already had gonorrhea a year ago when she was five." He paused, shook his head, and looked at Chris. "We've tried to help the woman . . . We tried to have the girl taken away from her, but we lost in the courts."

"How? How could you have lost?"

"You don't understand," Barrows said, suddenly impatient. "I'm going over to see the father and tell him where she is. He'll have to come for her."

"Has he been looking for her?"

"Not that I've heard. But I'm still going to see him. And this guy has a temper, so it'd be best all around if you turn over the girl and not say much."

Chris looked away.

"Okay?" he asked.

Chris nodded.

There were several seconds of silence while the two men looked at each other, as if they both wanted to say more. Then Barrows turned and walked down the stairs, and Chris went back into the apartment.

May was in the living room sitting on the floor rolling a beach ball back and forth with Lucy. The little girl remained on the edge of the rocker intently watching May and Lucy play. As he watched the girl, Chris felt a knot growing in the base of his throat and his back and shoulders grew stiff and uncomfortable. He knew May was waiting for his report, but he went into the bathroom and sat on the edge of the tub. He was staring at the wall when she came in the room.

"We have to just give her back," Chris said.

May seemed resigned. "I figured," she said. "That's always the way."

Chris said, "He's her father.

"Figures," she said, and she walked away.

Chris had already decided not to tell May the whole story. It would trouble her too much, and he knew her well enough to know she would appreciate being spared such details. He stood and looked at himself in the mirror. Then he joined May and the girls in the living room.

By seven-thirty, the man still hadn't come to pick up his daughter. May made dinner for the children and Chris tried to contact Child Welfare. He couldn't get through to that agency or any other, so he called the police and they told him to wait till morning and try again. Chris and May agreed to keep the girl overnight if the man didn't show. By ten o'clock Lucy had fallen asleep in May's arms, and the girl was dozing in front of the television, curled up on the rug. Chris was making up a bed in Lucy's room when the buzzer rang.

May was standing in the kitchen holding Lucy. The buzzer rang again and Chris went to the door and pressed the small black button that released the lock downstairs. Together they listened to him climb the stairs. Chris let him knock once before opening the door. He looked even bigger up close than he did from a distance, and Chris was surprised by his good looks. He had dark, neatly combed hair, and dark eyes. He looked like the kind of man you'd find in the advertising pages of a slick magazine.

"I've come to pick up my girl," he said. His voice was gentle and polite. He added, looking a bit awkward, "I appreciate your taking care of her."

Chris was encouraged by the man's manner. He didn't know what he had expected, but the man seemed shy and, except for his size, not threatening. "That's all right," Chris said. "She hasn't been any trouble." He moved out of the man's way, and pointed to the girl sleeping on the rug. "She's right there," he said, signaling that it was okay for him to go get her.

May took a step back as the man walked through the kitchen, and Chris followed him into the living room. Chris had expected him to wake the child, but instead he picked her up gently and carried her against his chest, the girl's head resting on his shoulder. In a kitchen doorway he turned again and said, "Thanks."

"She's a beautiful girl," Chris said. "She's always nicely dressed. She always looks pretty."

The man smiled, seemingly pleased by the compliment. "She does it herself," he said. "She's been like this since she could walk. She folds all her own clothes, and keeps everything neat in her dresser. She keeps the whole house clean. She's crazy like that. I don't know where she gets it from. Not me. And sure as hell not her mother."

"Oh," Chris said. He hesitated for a few moments, remembering the director's advice not to talk, but he was encouraged by the man's manner, so he continued. "I hope you won't mind my asking this," he said, "but she hasn't spoken to us. Is there something wrong? I mean, she seems bright and alert, but she just hasn't spoken."

The man nodded, looking at the floor. "She never talked," he said softly. "The doctor says there's nothing wrong with her, but . . ." He stopped and shook his head again and sighed. "It's her goddamn mother," he said bitterly. "The bitch is no good. She's screwed up my little girl's mind. She's no good." He looked up from the floor and for the first time looked at Chris directly. "Listen," he said. "I know what you must think of me, but that woman's a whore. She'd drive any man crazy. You understand?"

The man was looking at Chris as if he expected commiseration. Chris didn't know how to respond. He stared back, at a loss for words.

When Chris didn't answer, the man's face turned suddenly dark, and his free right hand contracted into a fist. "Sure," he said, still looking hard at Chris. "It's easy to judge. You got a little girl who can't talk?"

Again Chris didn't answer.

"Well? Have you, jerk?"

"Hey," Chris said. He meant to sound firm, but the word came out weak and childlike.

"Sure," the man said. "You shithead. What about your wife? She screw around on you?"

Chris took a step toward the man and said, this time firmly, "You'd better leave."

"Sure," he answered. Then he turned and looked at May and Lucy. "How do you think you'd feel," he said, "if something happened to your wife or your little girl?"

Chris raised his voice. "Get out of here!"

The man stared at Chris for another moment, intently, angrily, and then turned and walked out of the apartment, and as he started down the stairs Chris caught a glimpse of the child, her head still resting on his shoulder. He had thought she was asleep, since she had remained perfectly still in the man's arms, but when he saw her, her eyes were open and staring straight ahead, and her teeth were pressed together so hard that Chris could see the lines of tension running up through her cheeks to her temples. Her eyes seemed glazed and otherworldly in their stare, and combined with the tightness in her face, her appearance was so startlingly unnatural, so strikingly unlike the girl he saw every morning at the window, that he knew he would never forget the moment. That face would come up again and again in his memories and in his dreams.

When he closed the kitchen door his knees were weak. He turned to May and shook his head. May's face was calm, but he could see she was about to cry. For a moment he felt defensive, as if he needed to explain something, but he didn't know what there was to explain.

May carried Lucy off to bed. Chris went into the living room and sat in his rocker. He was waiting for May to come and join him, but as he sat and listened he heard her put Lucy in her crib and then cross the hallway to their bedroom. Then he heard the bed creak and he heard her sobbing, and he knew if he walked into the bedroom he'd see her lying on the bed with her head turned toward the wall, crying.

Chris sat back and looked around the room: at the three-piece sofa positioned nicely across from him, at the console stereo in the corner, at the aluminum and glass coffee table, and as he looked a terrible sense came over him that somehow gravity might fail and the furniture might shoot out of the room and fly away, like things sucked out of a vacuum. It was such an odd and new sensation that it made him smile and at the same time frightened him. In his head he heard himself thinking, "This is it, Chris. You're going crazy." Then his skin started to tingle and his forehead grew hot as he felt an absolute need to see himself from someplace outside of his body. It was crazy, but he felt as though he should be able to see himself from that perspective. One second he was frightened that he couldn't, the next he was frightened that he thought he could. "This is it," he heard another person in his mind repeating over and over. "This is it." And for a long while he sat silently in the living room, sweating, sure that he was losing his mind.

Then the fear just drifted away and was replaced by a heavy, heavy tiredness. He thought of that man in his kitchen, how in an instant his face had turned so dark as to look almost black. He thought of the mother and the little girl. In his tiredness, everything seemed terribly simple. In the morning he'd get up and go to work, and the little girl would be at the window. She'd wave to him and he'd wave back, and everything would continue just the same.

Chris stood and walked heavily and slowly to the bedroom, where he undressed and got into bed alongside May. He closed his eyes and in a moment found himself thinking of his house in the country. First he pictured the semicircular living room with its wall of glass, and then the small creatures, birds and squirrels, scurrying about the clearing. But, as hard as he tried, he couldn't make his mind's eye see that snow owl as it lifted itself into the air and filled the window with its wing span, and he couldn't, as hard as he tried, imagine what such a bird's great wings sounded like in flight. He drifted toward sleep envying the man who could, and went under, finally, his naked arm across the small of May's back, already dreaming of green mountains and pools of blue water surrounded by forests with nothing in them but trees and gentle animals and great white birds with wings that could fill a wall of glass full of sound and moving light.

HEART
ATTACKS

———————

The black guy must have spent one half of his life lifting
weights and the other half doing push-ups: when he moved
he threw the surface of his body into chaos, muscles scurried
out of each others' way, skin popped and bulged. He stared
intently, still as a cat, at a chunky white man with a beer belly
that hung over a fat leather belt and hair pulled into a ponytail that stuck out from the very top of his head. It was summer and both men were bare-chested. A girl dressed in pink
shorts and a pink halter sat on the sidewalk between them
with her chin resting on her knees, staring fixedly across the
street. Then the black man threw a punch that left the white
guy sprawled on the gray slate sidewalk. The girl turned to
look, then turned back and resumed her gaze. The black man
put his fists into the pockets of his white linen pants.

Tony let loose the slat of venetian blind he was peering
over, and it snapped back into place. He stepped away from

the window and stood in front of a full-length mirror attached to the sliding door of his bedroom closet. He was living in the second-floor apartment of a two-family house in Brooklyn. Behind him, he could see his bed and the girl lying on it. He couldn't remember whether her name was Gwen or Glenda, though they had met a dozen times on the elevator of the Mutual Building, where he worked on the sixty-fourth floor and she on the sixtieth. He said, "There's a fight on the street."

The girl turned on her stomach and buried her head in his pillow. "So?" she muttered. "In this neighborhood what's the surprise?" The sheets and pillowcases were white with a grid of black stripes. She looked like a squiggly line on graph paper.

Tony continued, silently, to examine himself in the mirror. On his thigh, he found a tiny brown spot he didn't remember having seen before, and his mouth went dry and his breathing grew shallow. For a month now he had stood naked in front of this mirror every morning and examined himself carefully. He had started doing this when he found a bright red spot on his chest and thought it might be a sign of cancer. The doctor told him it was a red spot and most people had them, and there was nothing at all to worry about. But he kept finding more and more spots—red spots, brown spots, black spots— and every time he found a new one, he saw Death looming beside him.

He sat on the edge of the bed and put his head down between his knees.

"I swear," the girl behind him said.

Tony took a deep breath, held it for ten seconds, then released it slowly.

"Will you just look at me?"

He turned toward her. She was sitting up with her legs folded under her in a way that would have ripped every ligament in his knees were he to try it. Her arms were crossed under her breasts.

"Look at me," she said.

Tony was looking at her knees. He looked up.

"There!" She jabbed a finger at his chest. "That's the first time! That's the first time since you took me here and did me like I was a blow-up doll that you've had the guts to look at me!" Her face crumpled and her bottom lip began to shake. "That's the first time."

"But I fell asleep after."

"That's right! That's just exactly right!"

Tony was silent for a moment. "Gwen," he said. "I—"

She jumped up and hit him in the face with her pillow. "Glenda, you bastard." She grabbed her clothes off the floor and began pulling them on.

"Glenda . . ." He rubbed his temples. "Glenda, I'm sorry. Truly. I'm nervous. I'm flying to San Francisco later to see my wife and kid."

Glenda stopped in the middle of pulling on a red leather boot.

"Ex-wife," Tony said. "Ex-wife and kid."

Silently, she continued dressing. She was quiet for a long time, and Tony sat awkwardly on the bed, resting his chin in the palm of his hand, unable to think of anything to say. Finally, she shook her head, as if resigned to a lousy fate, and asked, "How long you been divorced?"

"A little over a year."

"Who left who?"

"She left."

Glenda nodded. "Another man?"

Tony shook his head.

"How come you're going to see her?"

"My kid. Justin. I go to see my kid."

"Really. Why don't you just have her send him?"

"I don't know. We're still friends. I go to see her too."

"That's nice." Glenda pointed at the bed as she crossed the room to the window. "And that's the sacred place where you shared your great love."

"She's never seen this place. We had a nice house out in Riverhead before we split up."

Glenda pulled the venetian blinds open, looked out on the street and then closed them. "I don't see any fight out there."

Tony crawled over the bed and pulled the blinds up. The street was empty, and when he turned around the bedroom was empty too. "Glenda?"

The apartment door slammed.

He took another deep breath, and this time he listened to his heart. Lately, his heart had been doing funny things—skipping beats, jumping around, beating too fast and too loud. A few days ago, on the subway home from work, his heart started beating so wildly he was sure he was having a heart attack. When he reached his station, he was surprised to be alive. His heart seemed okay now, though maybe it was beating a little bit too loudly. He checked the time on the alarm clock and lay back on the bed, trying to be still so his heart would beat more softly. It was Saturday morning, three hours before he had to be at the airport. Three hours seemed like a very long time.

*   *

Allison looked out over the San Francisco Bay, and Tony straddled a chaise lounge. Allison was behind Tony, sitting quietly in a white rocking chair, protected from the sun by a baby blue umbrella that rose up out of the center of a round, marble table. She had a copy of the *American Book Review* in her lap and a lime and tonic in her hand. Justin was taking a nap inside, behind a pair of sliding glass doors.

Holding up a tumbler of bourbon, Tony gestured at his surroundings. "How does the guy manage this? He just lets you live here with Justin?" He was asking about Studs Reeger, the man who owned this house—Allison's editor, now that Allison was a poet.

Allison looked sad. "Why do you ask so many questions? Do I have to spell everything out for you? You're visiting for a few days; we have this place to ourselves. Why not just that simple?"

Tony thought about this. Reeger was a withered up old street bum who looked like he was a hundred years old, though he was probably only in his fifties. Allison was twenty-eight. When Tony met her, she was a slim girl with long blonde hair and bright blue eyes. Now her hair was short and slicked back in a stylish, modern cut. She was still slim, and he couldn't imagine her with Reeger. "Look," he said, "I'm just curious. I mean, this isn't the place you'd expect somebody who runs something called Black Bones Press to live, is it? I mean, you'd expect some inner-city hovel, wouldn't you?"

"Studs," Allison said, "happens to be a very wealthy man."

"This is the same guy I met at that gallery party? The drunk who kept farting and cursing?"

Allison stood up. "If you plan on being a bastard, you can leave right now."

"I don't mean anything," Tony said. "I mean, you're not living with this guy or anything, are you? You're not involved with him?"

"Good God. What do I have to do? Spell it out in block letters for you? I'm living with the man." She stood and went into the house.

Tony put his hands over his eyes. The last time he visited, she was living in a two-bedroom apartment with a girlfriend named Claire. He had always imagined her playing at the role of a struggling artist, and now, instead, he found her living in opulence with an old, foul-mouthed, flatulent drunk. He started for the house, but stopped when his fingers touched the handle of the sliding-glass door. He retook his seat on the chaise and tried to settle down.

Tony felt as though he was at a bad part of a bad dream that had begun years ago, when Justin was born. His life had been going along exactly as he wanted. He had a wife he loved, a job he liked: he was happy. The future he had always imagined—family gatherings with him at the head of the table, ocasional vacations, children and grandchildren—seemed possible, even probable. When the baby was born, he was happier than ever. Then, when Justin was only a few months old, Allison took up acting in local plays, leaving for rehearsals the minute Tony walked in the door from work. She started writing poetry—or what she called poetry. To Tony it looked like words arranged in patterns on the page, many of the words obscene. He thought she needed a therapist, and she thought he was old-fashioned. Then she started going to poetry readings in the city, and at one of them she met Claire, a woman who had published several books of poems. When, eventually, Claire read Allison's poetry, she wrote her a long letter about it, in which she said her poems were marked by the unmistakable voice of genius. Tony thought they both needed therapists. Claire introduced Allison to Reeger, and six months later Allison had a book in print. Then there was something every other night—parties, workshops, lectures, readings—and Allison seemed to grow younger and happier with every event. One night when Tony came home from work, he found a note on the table and an empty house.

When Allison came back out onto the terrace, she appeared to be angrier than she was when she went in. She positioned a chair directly in front of Tony and pointed at him. "You're a fool," she said. She had come back out of the house carrying a thick book under her right arm. She put it down carefully on the table. "You've always been. You left me alone in that morgue of a house out in the middle of nowhere twenty hours out of the day. It was like being dead out there. The most interesting thing you did was watch a PBS special. Our only stimulation was . . . What? Nothing. Sex, when you weren't too tired." She shook her head. "Leaving you was the smartest thing I ever did."

Tony got up and started for the stairs that led to the beach.

"You know what the worst thing was?"

Tony didn't want to know, but he asked anyway. "What?" He was standing with one hand on the wooden railing and his back turned to Allison. He watched two men walking arm in arm along the beach. One man laughed and kissed the other on the cheek. "What?" he repeated.

Allison's voice cracked. "You never looked at me. It was like you were blind."

Tony took a step, then stopped. "You're telling me this now? What about when it could have mattered?"

Allison closed her eyes. "You were hopeless. All you know is what you grew up with." She was crying.

"That's bullshit. That's not the whole story."

Allison said, "And what is?"

He continued down the stairs to the beach.

*   *

Allison came out of the back bedroom with Justin clinging to her leg. She was barefoot and wearing a pair of denims with a rough cotton pullover that had bright red stripes running diagonally across the front. Tony watched them from the living room, where he was sitting uncomfortably in a bean-bag chair. He had been watching a ball game on the forty-one-inch Sony that was mounted inside the living room wall. A sliding wood panel hid the set when it wasn't being used, which Allison claimed was most of the time.

Alongside the chair was something that looked like a chopping block and apparently served as an end table. A yellow pad and a gold Cross pen rested in the center of the board, and there was a slim book on top of the pad, titled *The George Washington Semen on Our Teeth*. Tony turned the book over when Allison sat Justin down in his lap.

"You're staying with Tony," Allison said to Justin.

Tony motioned toward the book. "You keep that kind of stuff in the living room."

Allison said, "It's an outrageous title, but he's a good poet."

Tony looked at her. "What happened to all those mysteries you used to read. You used to eat them up like candy."

"I don't like to think about those years. I was a different person then." She smiled and touched Justin on the belly. "I was in a state of suspended animation."

"You were alive anough to me."

She gave Tony a quick, serious look. "Don't start."

Tony put up his hands. Then he lowered an arm around Justin. "You and the old man are going to hang out tonight. We'll watch a ball game and drink some beer. What do you think?"

Justin looked up worriedly at his mother.

"You look nice," Tony said.

"Thanks." She pointed at the glass doors. "I'll be right next door if you need me. A few feet down the beach."

"What did you say the party was?"

"Just a party. She's a painter. She has lots of interesting friends."

Allison kissed Justin on the forehead and then tickled him under the arms.

Justin squealed and jumped.

Tony watched Allison leave and listened to the soft footfall of her bare feet on the stairs. When she had been gone a few minutes, he turned to Justin and asked, "Well, Tiger! What's the story? What do you want to do?"

Justin seemed to think about this for a while. He said, "Justin tired. Justin wants go to bed." He got up out of the bean-bag chair and toddled sadly down the hall to his bedroom.

Tony followed and tucked him in. "Hey, Big Guy," he said. "You sure you don't want to stay up and play with Daddy awhile?"

Justin shook his head and turned over.

"Okay," Tony said. He leaned in and kissed his son on the cheek. "Daddy will see you in the morning." He left the room, closing the door only halfway so he could hear if Justin called. Then he switched the television off in the living room and went out onto the terrace. The night had turned cloudy and windy, and as Tony leaned against the railing, looking out over the water, wind pushed his hair back off his forehead and whistled in his ears. He turned the chaise around so that its raised back blocked the wind. It also faced the house where the party was going on; and through the living room windows, he could see the guests mingling, though he couldn't see Allison. He turned away from the party and looked down the long expanse of beach. Then he closed his eyes.

Tony's father had been a big, tough man. A first-generation Italian who made a living as a mason. He never made a lot of money, and he wasn't especially generous; but his children always had what they needed. Family and work, that was all the man knew. That was all that mattered. Tony could only remember one compliment from his father, and that came when he was a senior in high school. He was an average kid— average height, average build—with a dark complexion. He wasn't handsome, but he wasn't ugly either. In his senior year he joined the wrestling team, and after several months of daily workouts, his physique changed, becoming thick and muscular. One afternoon his father, who had always been a burly man given to wearing armless T-shirts, nodded at him and said he was looking good.

That was the only compliment Tony could remember. His father was not given to statements of affection or praise. When the old man was dying, his body reduced to pallid skin and sharp bones, his hair gone and the shape of his face changed by the drugs he had been taking, Tony had tried to tell him something. The hospital room was thick with the smell of antiseptics. It was December and a fake, foot-high Christmas tree with red and green lights blinked on and off in the plate-glass window beside his father's bed. He had a tube in his nose and another in his arm, and he was only a few hours away from dying. Tony leaned close to him and said what he had never said before. He whispered, "I love you, Dad." His father's response was to look up and shake his head disapprovingly, as if Tony had breached some code of conduct. Tony patted him on the leg and left the room feeling ashamed.

At the funeral he held his mother up when her legs buckled; and when the coffin lid was closed, and his mother screamed, he held his arm fast around her shoulder and helped her back to the waiting limousine. That was years ago. Now his mother was dead too, and since the divorce he had drifted away from his remaining family.

Behind him, the wind knocked a heavy, glass flowerpot off the terrace railing, and it broke into several pieces when it hit the deck. Tony looked at it, and considered cleaning up the mess and finding another pot; but instead, he went back into the house and checked on Justin. The child was sleeping soundly. He looked snug and warm, cuddled up under a thick, blue comforter decorated by a variety of Sesame Street characters. Justin's hand lay peacefully on Oscar the Grouch's head. Tony left the room, closing the door behind him, and he went back out onto the terrace. He looked down at the plant lying on its side with its pale, ugly roots exposed. The wind was blowing harder now. He looked into the house where the party was going on, and he saw Allison in the living room: her bare feet stood out against the bright-red carpeting. She was absentmindedly pushing her hair back behind her ear as she spoke to a boyish looking character with shoulder-length platinum-blond hair and a big, bright-orange bow tie. Tony looked at the black bean-bag chair for a moment, then walked down the stairs and crossed the beach to the party.

Several guests had congregated on the windy terrace, and Tony nodded politely to them as he passed by. Inside, a Talking Heads song was playing softly through speakers hidden someplace in the ceiling. He looked over to where Allison was still involved with the blond-haired boy; then he stepped into the circle of a conversation going on between two men and an attractive, young girl wearing a denim miniskirt and a sheer red blouse. One of the men was black and dressed in jeans and a faded work shirt, and the other, a white man, was wearing a sport jacket with a tan shirt and a white knit tie. Tony had trouble following the conversation, and he watched the girl, whom he learned was a student, as she listened intently, hanging on their every word. They were talking about golden showers, and all Tony could figure out from their talk was that they were in essential agreement about something.

"Excuse me," Tony said, "I hate to seem ignorant—but what's a golden shower?"

The circle went silent for a moment, and then the white man said, "It's a form of sexual behavior in which one person urinates on the other."

Tony's mouth fell open. When he realized how dumb he must look, he hurried to say something. "That's . . . That's not healthy, is it?"

"Well, there are lots of stipulations here," the man touched his white knit tie hesitantly, "but, on the whole, no, I don't think it's healthy."

The black man shrugged. "I don't agree." He looked into Tony's eyes. "I see it as another manifestation of desire. Another flow of sexual energy." He laughed at himself. "Excuse the pun. It wasn't intended."

The girl giggled.

Tony said, "Sure. But couldn't you say the same thing about murder?"

The man took a step back. "That's an asinine comparison." He looked tremendously angry, as if he were considering throwing a punch. Then he just walked away.

The other man put his arm around the girl's waist and led her off.

Tony crossed the room to Allison. She was still listening to the blond kid when he came up behind her and put his hand on her shoulder.

Allison turned around with a big smile, but when she saw who it was, the smile disappeared and her eyes flashed the way they always did when she was angry. "What are you doing here?" she asked. Then she added quickly, "Who's with Justin?"

"Justin's okay. I came over because the wind knocked your plant off the terrace rail."

"That's why you're here?"

The boy touched her on the shoulder. He said, "I'll talk to you later, Allie," and joined another group of people across the room.

"Allie? Is that what they call you?"

"Are you going back, or do I have to leave the party?"

"I'm going back. If you tell me where another pot is, I'll take care of the plant."

"Don't worry about it."

From where Tony was standing he could see the back side of a partition that divided the living room. Hanging on it was a massive painting of a totally nude, bulky, angry-looking woman with her fist raised in the old black power salute of the sixties and seventies. The colors were garishly bright, and on the whole the piece reminded Tony of the kind of art he saw painted on the walls in news stories about communist or totalitarian states. It looked like it should be the face of Lenin or that guy who ran North Korea. "Is that socialist art, or something like that?" Tony asked, sincerely, pointing at the painting.

Allison said, "That painting's worth more than you'll earn in the next five years."

Tony took a step back and looked at her. This was a woman he had known for ten years, had lived with for eight, had considered himself so intimately joined with that nothing could ever tear them apart. He touched her on the shoulder and said, "Hey. Fuck you." He left the party, and this time when he crossed the terrace, the people gathered there stared at him.

He went back to Allison's house and after checking on Justin, he turned off all the lights and sat on the floor by the sliding-glass doors. He watched the wind chopping at the surface of the ocean. He listened to it howl through the cracks in the house and thought about nothing at all. He sat there quietly for a long time looking and listening. Then he pulled himself to his feet and slid the glass door fully open, so that the cold wind raced past him into the house. Behind him, he heard something fall and break, but he didn't turn to see what it was. He leaned out the door, into the wind, and felt it harsh against his face; and he had to squint to keep his eyes open, to keep looking. He gritted his teeth and felt the wind in his mouth; he lowered his head, and the wind on his scalp felt like fingers pushing his hair up and back. Then he took off his shirt and undershirt, and he could feel the wind against his chest. He could feel it down to his guts and in his balls, and for a moment he considered taking off the rest of his clothes. Then Allison appeared on the terrace looking sad. She came into the house, closed the door, and sat down on the floor.

"It's dark in here."

Tony sat in front of her so that his knees were touching her knees. He said, "I turned off the lights."

She pushed her hair off her forehead. "I'm truly sorry for what I said—about the painting, and money."

Tony nodded.

"That was cruel and stupid. I'm not like that. You know I'm not like that."

"I know." Tony held his head in his hands. He said, "You know how if I were sick or scared about something, the way you used to hold me? Sometimes we'd take off our clothes and just lie there for a long time?"

Allison looked down. "It's not like it happened once a week."

"But you remember?"

"Of course, I remember."

He put his hand on her knee. "Could you do that again for me? One more time?"

She shook her head.

"Okay," Tony said. "I understand. It's just that . . . something's wrong with me. Something's happening to me. I'm sure of it. I'm absolutely positive."

"What? What are you talking about?"

"I've got these spots turning up on me. It's like they're a sign of something."

"What kind of spots?"

"Red spots, brown spots, black spots, you name it."

Allison leaned closer to him. "I don't see any spots."

"It's dark in here."

"I didn't see any spots before either."

"They're on my chest mostly, and my legs."

"Have you seen a doctor?"

"I went to Taylor."

"What did he say?"

Tony shrugged. "Nothing. He said they were nothing. If they're nothing, how come they keep turning up like this?"

"Maybe they're just birthmarks and moles and junk. You're just noticing them because you're looking for them."

"That's what Taylor said."

Allison was quiet for a long time. Then she asked, "How long has this been going on?"

"Months," Tony said. "This, and my heart's been acting up too, acting weird. I think they're connected somehow. I can feel it."

"Tony, don't be insulted by this or anything, but I think maybe you should see a psychiatrist, or a therapist."

"I'm not insulted. You're probably right. I know you're right."

"You might try the guy you pissed off at the party. He's supposed to be good."

Tony looked surprised. "That guy's nuts."

"He's going around asking everybody who you are. I told him I had no idea. Never saw you before in my life."

"The guy was saying . . ." He thought about how he might explain what the guy was saying; then he waved it off as if it weren't worth the effort. "I don't care what people do with each other, what they do to each other. In bed, I mean. I don't care if they sleep with snapping turtles. It doesn't matter." He pointed to Allison. "But that doesn't make it normal. That doesn't mean it's healthy."

Allison threw her hands up. "What? What's normal, Tony? What's healthy? You mean, what's normal and healthy for you is normal and healthy for everybody?"

"God damn. Can't you just agree, even if you don't?"

Allison shook her head.

"Fine." He stood. "I'm tired. I'm going to bed." He started for the guest room, where his unpacked suitcase lay at the foot of a king-size bed.

"Good night," Allison said.

Tony nodded.

As he got undressed, he hung his clothes on a sculpture that was composed principally of mangled bicycle parts, mangled animal forms, and garbage. When he was in his pajamas and under the covers, Allison knocked and came into the room.

"Did you change your mind?" Tony asked.

"About what?"

"I didn't think so." He turned onto his back. "What is it?"

"I don't think," Allison said, "you should stay the whole time. It's not working out."

Tony looked at the bicycle sculpture, at a wormy, half-rotted apple impaled on a bent spoke. He muttered, "Shit. I just traveled . . ." Then he stopped. He was tired. He was sleeping in some other guy's bedroom—some guy who could buy and sell him. "Fuck it," he thought. He said, "Okay. Whatever you want. I'll leave tomorrow afternoon. That way I won't lose any pay. Hey," he added, as if it had just occurred to him, "you going to marry this guy Reeger so I can stop paying through the nose?"

Allison stepped back into the doorway. "I haven't touched your money in months. It goes straight into an account for Justin. I'll show you the passbook in the morning."

"Okay," Tony said. "That's fine."

Allison started to close the door, then stopped. "Tony," she said softly, "are you seeing anybody else? Have you got somebody to . . . somebody special?"

"Sure," Tony said. "A girl named Gwen. She's very pretty. Very nice. Gentle, soft-spoken. Too young for me though. Much younger than us."

"Well," Allison said, "but you have somebody."

"Sure. You didn't think I'd be sleeping alone, did you?"

She laughed. "No. Of course not." She started to close the door again. "Well, I'll see you in the morning then."

When the door clicked shut, Tony lay still and quiet, staring at the ceiling.

*   *

Monday morning it rained, and as always on rainy days, there were bums in the subway station. Three of them were at the back of the platform, and the whole station stank with their damp, foul odor. A tall, skinny bum in a felt hat stood a few feet from the corner where a man and a woman were huddled close under a bright green tarp that looked as if it had just come off somebody's new sports car. The man, unshaven, with a purplish-red welt under his eye and a fresh gash on his forehead, was sound asleep with his head resting on the woman's breasts. The woman was awake, and she patted the grimy bum's shoulder as she stared out into nothing as peacefully and calmly as if she were in her own bedroom.

Tony leaned against a brick column and looked down the dark tracks, anxious for the train to arrive. Among the dozen commuters waiting with him was an old woman who leaned on her umbrella as if it were a cane. She kept coughing and putting her hand up over her nose. She looked up at Tony, obviously pleased to be standing next to a well-dressed man. She whispered, "Stinks in here, don't it?" and she jerked her head toward the bums.

Tony looked at the bums again, and the beat-up one under the tarp made a soft, sleepy sound and nuzzled closer to the woman, who patted his hair and kissed his wound, as if her kiss might heal it. Before he realized what he was doing, Tony crossed the platform and kicked the sleeping bum in the sole of his foot. Then he kicked at the woman's feet too, and over their yowls of protest, he screamed, "Get out of here, you lousy bums!"

The bum who had been standing against the wall lunged at Tony, and Tony hit him flat on the nose with his fist. The man groaned deeply and backed up holding his face in his hands.

From behind Tony, one of the other commuters leaped forward brandishing his umbrella and yelling, "Come on, you stinking bums! You want trouble!"

The old woman scurried up to Tony and handed him her umbrella. Tony waved it over his head. "Get out of here!" he screamed. "You better get out of here!"

The bums grouped together and walked slowly along the back wall of the station, and then quietly up the stairs and out into the rain. The woman who had been holding the beat-up bum under the tarp, turned around on the street and called down into the station, sadly, "You mad peoples. You ter'ble mad peoples."

The commuters all laughed at her. All except Tony, who was frightened now because his heart was beating way way too fast and too loudly. He was afraid he was going to have a heart attack right there.

The commuter who had aided Tony patted him on the back. "Nice going, Bud," he said. "We don't need them stinking bums down here, do we?"

Tony nodded and tried to smile.

"What's a'matter?" the old woman asked. "You okay? You look pale."

"I'm okay," Tony said, and he walked stiffly away from them. He wanted to be alone so he could be still and quiet. He tried breathing regularly and calmly, but still his heart raced.

When the train pulled into the station, he stepped into a car feeling weak. He took a seat next to an old woman reading the *New York Post*. On the cover was a picture of a partly nude man in midair, falling to his death against the background of a burning building. His robe was on fire and it unfurled behind him like wings in flame. Tony tried to concentrate on the ugly graffiti that covered every inch of the train car. He saw spray-painted names and words and shapes, and it appeared to him unsalvageably ugly and offensive. It felt like thousands of rude, angry people shouting for his attention. He looked hard, though, for what might be beautiful in it, having read articles in papers and magazines that argued for graffiti as art. The more he concentrated, the more the bright, ugly letters and shapes seemed to jump off the walls at him, and when he arrived at the station his heart was still beating hard and fast. He didn't think it could keep up like this much longer without failing. He climbed the steps out of the subway and walked the two city blocks to the Mutual Building feeling shaky, ready any second for the wicked pressure in his chest that would signal an attack.

In the crowded express elevator on the way up to his office, he felt his left arm growing numb and tingly, a symptom, he had read, which immediately preceded heart attacks. His breathing grew shallow and he slumped a little to the side, and when he did so, he found himself pushing against Glenda, the back of his arm touching her breasts. When he felt the contact and saw who it was, he thought his heart beat slowed down a little bit and began to beat more regularly. "Hi," he said, breathlessly. "Hello."

Glenda nodded at him.

He was quiet for the rest of the ride, but he didn't move, as he could have, to avoid the contact of his arm against her breast. He stayed precisely where he was, staring at the elevator doors, and when they arrived at the sixtieth floor and Glenda yanked herself away from him, he said, "Gwen, I'd like to see you again, if you want."

Glenda turned, framed by the open doors, and said slowly, "When you die, maybe we'll see each other in heaven. Before then, I hope never to see your face, or any other part of you." The doors closed. After that, it was so quiet in the elevator, Tony was sure everybody could hear his heart beating, for now it was beating as wild and fast as it was right after the incident with the bums. On the sixty-fourth floor, he stepped out of the elevator and crossed the office to his desk. When he sat down, he was glassy eyed and his heart was still pounding.

A fellow office worker, a guy Tony had drinks with sometimes, came over to his desk carrying a cup of coffee. He had been on the elevator. "Hey," he said, "Don't let her get to you. She's just some bitch." He put the coffee down on the desk, patted Tony on the shoulder, and walked away.

Tony wasn't embarrassed by Glenda. He was afraid he was about to die. His heart beat crazily, so crazily he feared it couldn't possibly keep up much longer: in a few seconds, in a few minutes, it just had to seize. He crossed his hands on the desk, wrist over wrist, and tried to be calm. Outside, the morning sun shone red on the windows of the adjacent skyscraper, and Tony found himself strangely attracted to the bright, reflected light. It had made the building look, in the first moment when he had noticed, as if it were wrapped in flames. He walked to the window and pressed the palms of his hands flat against the glass. The surrounding buildings seemed different somehow, changed. People crowded the streets, and there was something so frightening about how small and distant they appeared, that he began to sweat. He told himself that he wasn't dying, that it was all in his head, that this was not the end, and he went on reassuring himself, his hands pushing against the cold glass and his heart beating wildly, as throngs of people flowed along the street like a dark river, fast and deep. Under his feet he could feel the whole building moving, as if it were being rocked by the current of that river, as if the whole city had started to tremble.

SIR THOMAS
MORE
IN THE
HALL OF
LANGUAGES

—————————

Robert Knott's eyebrows grew together thickly over the bridge of his nose so that they formed an oblique v and looked like dark wings spread in flight about to carry him away. Where they met the hair grew confused and disordered, and Robert had to comb it back over his eyes each morning as best he could. Growing up, he hated his eyebrows. They made him the butt of jokes and got him into fights. Now, even with a wife who claimed to like his hirsute brow, he still occasionally grew angry at his appearance. He felt that nature, by so small a thing as letting his eyebrows grow together, had ruined an otherwise handsome face.

This evening they were particularly bothersome. He stood in front of the bathroom mirror and scowled as he primped, preparing for his evening class. Though he made his living as a corporate officer, he had earned a Ph.D. in philosophy. There was nothing, however, one could do with a degree in philosophy other than teach philosophy; and since teaching wasn't nearly lucrative enough for Robert's tastes, he went back to school, this time to study business management. He had not yet—now in his mid-forties—reached the lap of luxury, but he was on his way. He lived in DeWitt, a mostly wealthy suburb of Syracuse, in an expansive colonial house with his wife and two children—who were in Florida for the week visiting his wife's parents.

For two years he had been teaching a basic course in the history of philosophy for Syracuse University. He was officially on their faculty as an adjunct instructor, which was a good deal for him and the University. The school got a qualified teacher for minimal cost, and Robert got to keep in touch with philosophy and to see a lot of young, pretty girls. He especially liked the girls. His wife, attractive when he married her, had grown matronly. He had watched the change come over her slowly, and now, after seventeen years of marriage, she just wasn't the same person he had married. Their sex life, strong at the start, had turned skinny and ragged. Still, his life could have been more exciting, but it seemed basically sound; and he never seriously thought of leaving his wife—which is not to say he didn't think of other women.

In fact, he always thought of other women. He admired them wherever he could find them—on the beach, at a picnic, at the park. He ogled their naked bodies nightly on pay TV, and he enjoyed fantasizing about affairs. Fantasizing, Robert reasoned, was healthy and even moral. It kept his sex life alive and thus kept him from fooling around.

Robert wet his finger in the warm water, brought it to the bridge of his nose, and—with no success—tried to smooth his unruly eyebrows. Finally, he gave up and left the bathroom. He turned off the house lights and started for the car. His class met once a week on Tuesday nights, and last week he had made a point to tell his students that his wife and children were in Florida for a two-week vacation. He did this because one of the girls in his class, Alicia, had been flirting with him all semester. He didn't really expect anything to happen, but it was part of his fantasy life to play such games.

Alicia was bright. She was nineteen and came from a wealthy family, and though she was not particularly pretty, she was young and trim and attractive in her way. In class, she tried to attract Robert's attention. She always went braless, often wearing blouses that showed flashes of skin. When she wore skirts, she let them slide up on the thighs. Once, when taking an exam—Robert still wasn't sure if she was conscious of this or not—she slouched down in her chair and propped her feet up on the seat in front of her; and with her knees resting comfortably against the seat's backrest, she casually wrote her exam. Robert stared up her skirt, at sheer red panties. That vision had perked up his sex life for months. Robert appreciated Alicia and he thanked her by inflating her grades, though they hardly needed it; and he always made a point of saying something nice to her after class.

Inside the front doors of the Hall of Languages, he stopped and shook off the cold. It was an average December night in Syracuse, near the end of the fall semester, and he had just hurried across the snow- and ice-covered grounds from his distant parking space. The Hall of Languages was the oldest building on campus, and the wooden floor creaked beneath his weight. There were plans underway to renovate the building's interior, but for now the absurdly high ceilings and the ornate wooden doors with thick glass panes remained. Robert blew his nose, straightened out his hair, and for one last time tried to smooth the hair over his nose; then he mounted the spiral staircase that formed the centerpiece of the building and climbed to his third-floor classroom.

The first few minutes of class were ritualistic. He placed his books on the desk, carefully removed his jacket and hung it over the back of his chair, and read the class roll. Then he stepped around to the front of the desk and for the first time looked up at the students. This was the signal that class was to begin.

Robert was pleased to see Alicia sitting in the front row. She was wearing a plum-colored skirt that buttoned down the side, and a soft, brown velour pullover. He glanced quickly at her legs. "Well," he said. "Here's a class of experts on Sir Thomas More."

Most of the students laughed.

Robert raised his eyebrows. "You've all read—have you not?—a selection of his writing, including all of *Utopia.*"

A few nodded.

"Which means you know more about More than most." Robert smiled.

"Poor Sir Thomas," Alicia said.

"Well," he continued. "Who'll tell me something about Sir Thomas?"

From the back of the classroom a dark-haired athlete said, "He was a saint."

"And? Why?"

"Because he wouldn't support Henry the Eighth's break from the Roman Catholic Church, and Henry had him beheaded. So the church made him a saint."

Robert nodded. "What else?" The class was silent. "Come on," he prodded. "What else do you know about Sir Thomas More?"

Someone said: "He's dead."

The class laughed. "Beyond the obvious," Robert continued, "what else do you know?"

One of his weaker students raised her hand. "His most famous book," she said, "is *Utopia,* which I really like a great deal. It shows a blueprint for a perfect society, which More believed was possible."

Robert frowned. "Did he? Did he think a perfect society possible?"

The girl looked uncertain, but nodded.

"Don't you think it odd," Robert asked her, "that as devout a Catholic as Saint Thomas More would have advocated such things in his perfect society as euthanasia, the marriage of priests, divorce by mutual consent because the couple no longer liked each other? Or, on another level, didn't you think it odd that the residents of Utopia used golden chamber pots?"

The girl looked confused.

From the back of the room, the athlete spoke up. "Maybe it's odd," he said. "But it didn't seem to me that *Utopia* was supposed to be a satire or anything."

Robert didn't respond. Alicia raised her hand and he pointed to her.

"H. W. Donner," she said, "suggests that More wanted the

reader to see the absurdity of trying to attain perfection on earth. His point was that earthly institutions can never be perfect. Christians can only expect to find perfection in heaven, and if they want to achieve heaven, and make a better world for themselves while on earth, they should try to rid themselves of the passions that are at the root of evil."

Robert looked impressed, and nodded appreciatively.

The class was quiet for a moment; then the athlete raised his hand, as did two other students, ready to disagree with Alicia, H. W. Donner be damned. Robert pointed to one of the boys, and then relaxed and leaned back against his desk. He could see that a discussion was about to begin. From here on, his job would be to direct the talk into profitable channels.

The class turned out to be lively, and when it was over Alicia loitered in her seat until all the other students had left. Then she walked to the desk, where Robert was gathering his books.

"You were sharp tonight," he said. "Do you especially like More?"

She shook her head. "Do you?"

Robert shook his head, and they both laughed.

"What are you doing now?" she asked.

Robert was taken aback by her question. He felt a warm flush run along his skin as he hesitated awkwardly and pressed his thumb against the bridge of his nose, an old habit from adolescence that he thought he had completely broken.

"I just thought," Alicia continued, "that if you weren't in a hurry you might give me a ride home. My apartment's on Euclid Avenue."

"Oh sure," Robert said, resuming his professorial tone. He put his hand on her shoulder and pointed her to the door.

Outside, they hurried through the parking lots to his car. Robert unlocked the passenger's door for her, and then hurried around to the driver's side. Once in the car, he pumped the gas and started the engine. The car was a late-model Cadillac Seville.

Alicia looked surprised. "This does not," she said, "look like a prof's car."

"It's not," Robert said.

"You must be a hot shot at your other job."

"What other job? Teaching is something I do one night a week. My real work is with new technologies."

"Oh," Alicia said, "that's interesting." She turned and noticed there were two thick blankets in the back seat. "Professor Knott," she said, as if surprised. "What are those blankets doing in the back seat?"

At first Robert was confused; then he blushed. Her tone gave him the perfect opportunity to say something suggestive—but he couldn't think. "I'm supposed to drop them in a Salvation Army box."

"Does your wife like giving things to charity?" she asked. Then she pointed to the house on the right side of the street. They were almost at the end of Euclid Avenue. "That's my place," she said.

Robert pulled over. The lights were on in the second-story windows.

"Damn," she said. "My roommate's home."

"Don't you get along with your roommate?"

"She's okay. Didn't you tell our class something about your wife's roommate in college?"

During their college years, his wife's roommate was jealous of her. Whenever Robert came to call, the roommate managed to do something rude, until he stopped visiting. For dates, he would call in advance and his future wife would meet him on the porch. He remembered how she looked then, how anxious she was to see him; and he remembered the excitement of those nights, nights that promised hard-won sex and passion. "Yes," he said. "They didn't get along."

"What did you do," she asked, "when you wanted to see her, but her roommate was there?"

"What do you mean?"

"I mean, if her roommate was home, and you didn't want to go up."

"Oh," Robert said. "Usually we'd just drive."

"Let's go for a drive then," she said, and she turned quickly in her seat and looked straight ahead.

Robert hesitated.

"Come on," she said. "Where did you go?"

142

"Looking at houses, mostly," he answered.

"Looking at houses?"

"We'd drive and look at the most expensive houses in town."

"Oh, like dreaming of living there yourself one day." Alicia seemed to like that idea. "Come on," she said. "I know a mansion on the west side of town, behind Onondaga Park. Let's go check it out."

Robert turned and for the first time looked hard at Alicia. She had let her skirt ride up on her thighs, and now she crossed her legs and tapped his calf with her heel and smiled seductively. He looked down at her legs, where the soft white skin disappeared under the plum skirt. He put the car in gear.

*   *

Parked outside a dark mansion, lying under the blankets in the back seat, Alicia's naked body sleeping curled against his, Robert stared happily at the bright stars through the car's rear window. The other windows were covered with condensation, but the electric defrost quietly kept the rear window clear, and Robert felt as vibrant and alive as the sky he watched glittering above him. They were parked outside a wrought iron gate that separated the public park from the private mansion. Robert, directed by Alicia, had had to take a dirt road off the park's main circle to get there. When they arrived, all the windows in the house were dark. He backed the car as close to the gate as possible before they climbed into the rear seat to get a better look. Once in the back seat, they forgot about the mansion. Now he recognized the structure only as shadow that rose up behind the car and blocked off part of his view of the night sky.

Robert thought of all the times he had warned himself against this kind of thing, and he felt stupid. He had always imagined that after the fling he would feel guilty, but there was none of that at all. He felt good. He felt happy to be alive. Carefully, he lifted the top blanket to look down at Alicia's body. His own body annoyed him. He was fat and out of shape and reminded himself of a lumbering bear; but her body was tight and firm. As he stared at the soft skin of her breasts pressed against his chest, he felt his heartbeat start once again to accelerate. Then a light came through the back window.

Robert jumped into a sitting position and pulled the blankets to his chest. He imagined there was a policeman outside shining a flashlight into the car, but as he looked out the window he saw, with some relief, that that wasn't it at all. A boy dressed in a black suit had turned on the lights in a kitchen the size of three ordinary kitchens and was rummaging through the refrigerator. Robert watched him through a huge bay window. From where the car was situated, some twenty or twenty-five feet from the building, slightly above and to the right of the window, Robert could see into the kitchen so clearly that the boy in black looked like an actor performing on a stage.

Alicia sat up and looked out from under the blankets.

"I almost had a heart attack," Robert whispered.

"You think he can see us?" she asked.

Robert shook his head. "It's dark out here and light in there. He'd have to press his nose against the window and look for us."

Alicia watched as the boy returned, empty handed, to the kitchen table and sat down. He looked as though he had been sleeping in his clothes: his jacket and pants were crumpled and his hair was pressed flat on one side of his head. The boy folded his arms upon the table and rested his cheek against one wrist. His eyes were open and his head was turned toward the window, so that he was looking out at the darkness, but to Robert and Alicia it looked as though he were staring at them. Then his body began to heave and shake, and they could see he was crying. As they watched, an older woman entered the kitchen. She too was dressed in black clothes that were disheveled—the seams of her dark nylons were twisted, and a middle button of her black blouse was undone. She pulled a chair up by the boy and lay her head on the back of his neck. She joined the boy in looking out the window, but seemed too tired and drawn out to cry. She just stared vacantly at the darkness.

"Let's get out of here," Alicia said. "It's like they're looking at us."

They won't be up long," Robert said. "If I start the car they'll notice us."

Alicia looked at him. "Afraid they'll call the police?"

He shrugged. Then he stroked her hair and kissed her on the forehead. "It looks like somebody died," he said. "It's spooky."

They looked again to the window, and as they did an elderly man walked slowly into the kitchen, followed by two teenage boys. All three sat at the table. The woman smiled at them and the boy stopped crying, but he didn't look up. Then another woman and a teenage girl walked in, and they too sat at the table.

"This is getting to be a party," Robert said.

"It's eerie," Alicia said. "My father just died."

"I'm sorry," Robert said. He was surprised. "When did he die?"

"A few months ago. Just before the semester started."

"I'm sorry," he repeated. "I don't think you've mentioned it before."

"He was a bastard anyway. I hated him. He left me and my mother when I was just a kid, and I only saw him a couple of times a year. I don't even think he liked me."

"Still . . ." Robert didn't know how to continue.

"Do you believe this?" Alicia asked.

Two men had just joined the others at the table, and now another woman entered the room. She was old, but spry and she seemed more to jump than walk into the room. She said something as she came in that made the boy look up from the table and smile, and then she said something else that made everyone laugh. In the car, Robert and Alicia could hear the laughter. It was loud and it went on a good while.

Robert felt naked and uncomfortable. "Let's get dressed," he said, and he and Alicia started gathering their clothes.

While Robert and Alicia struggled in the cramped and dark back seat of the car, the women in the kitchen busied themselves around the stove and refrigerator, under the animated direction of the elderly woman. She pointed to the stove, and one of the young girls put on a pot of coffee. She pointed to the refrigerator, and another girl started making sandwiches; and when Robert and Alicia looked up again, the scene in the kitchen had changed entirely. Now, instead of one boy alone crying, there was a rush of activity, with sandwiches being placed on the table, and coffee cups and platters coming down from the cupboards. Now everyone was talking, and the boy who only a moment ago was crying, was holding a sandwich in his hand, about to take a bite, and laughing at something one of the teenage girls had said.

In the back seat of the car, Robert and Alicia huddled down under their blankets, watching and waiting for it all to be over. It was cold in the car, but Robert was nervous and he felt flushed and incredibly hot—as if, somehow, the car were an inferno and the blanket a robe of flames.

ST. AUGUSTINE
ON
MONY
TOWER

"Of faith and man," the Bishop of Hippo was saying; "Of free will and the immortality of souls," he said, standing on MONY Tower, overlooking the city of Syracuse. Strand had not yet reached the roof, still climbing as he was the dense copper stairs flight after flight, but he could see St. Augustine dressed in white robes atop the black tower, his hands extended in benediction, the wind wimpling and snapping his vestments, and though the bishop spoke into the wind, Strand could hear him clearly. His voice was in fact like music.

But no meaning lingered: the words came, resolved, and disappeared, frustrating Strand, hungry not for sound but message. At the eighteenth floor on the final landing he pulled open the last door and saw before him a great black expanse. For a second. Then one wall flashed, in massive figures, backwards, in bright lights: 22°. Then darkness. Then the time: 3:57. Then darkness. And so it went as Strand peered into the clock room: temperature, darkness, time, darkness, temperature—

And it will go on like this forever, Strand thought, ad infinitum.

So it had been flashing the time and temperature fifteen years ago when he first came to Syracuse, a bright student beginning graduate study in the history of religions at Syracuse University, driving a beat-up '68 Ford heading north on Route 81 from Long Island, where he had just completed a B.A. in Anthropology at Hofstra College. He was twenty-one then. He was driving without a license from his parents' house in Cold Spring Harbor. After Binghamton and a fifty mile stretch of hills and farmland, Syracuse appeared before his eyes as a great metropolis. On his left he saw the twin towers of MONY Plaza. Though they were not the tallest buildings in the skyline—a circular Holiday Inn nearby was taller, and two or three other buildings were at least the same height— the two black towers stood out because of their proximity and symmetry, and of the two towers the one bearing the MONY name and logo dominated because it bore also the huge digital clock and thermometer by which Syracusans checked the time and weather.

How many mornings driving up Adams on his way to campus had he checked his time against the time on MONY Tower, craning in the morning rush-hour traffic?

"Syracusans are a punctual lot," he said, watching the door to the clock room close slowly behind him. "They take time seriously in Syracuse." Then he realized that he no longer heard the saint's voice or saw his image, though now, in the clock room, he was closer to him than ever.

He turned around and it was dawn and he was returning from a business trip driving up the steep hill on Colvin Avenue after having spent the night in another city with another woman. He was on his way home and it was snowing slightly and the studded snows on his late-model car ripped up the ice and snow on the ground and carried him easily up the hill. It was a magnificent dawn: it had snowed hard all night and the snow had cleansed everything. It weighed heavily on the trees, bending the branches. Snow and ice hanging from rooftops made the dawn bright and comforting, and Strand was warm in the driver's seat when he made a sharp right-hand turn into his driveway. But the driveway had not been shoveled and the car faltered on the incline, the spinning of the rear wheels making a whistling noise that sizzled along the street. Strand cursed his boy John for not having shoveled the drive, and his wife for not having made him. The boy will be thirteen soon, he thought, and should learn to accept responsibility.

He got out of the car and left it running. He could feel the arctic cold air in his mouth and nose and eyes as he walked up the driveway to the garage for a snow shovel. The snow squeaked under his shoes. And there was his son John sitting up behind the juniper bush, frozen. Strand looked at him for a long time. The boy was sitting up straight, his legs extended along the ground, his torso forming a right angle to his legs. His skin was bluish white and covered with a light dusting of snow. A string of fluid was frozen in a thick line from his shirt collar to the corner of his mouth, where it distorted the shape of his upper lip. His eyes were closed. Strand touched him and the body was frozen to the ground. It didn't move.

Strand heard a great noise in the clock room and when he looked for the source he saw the stage at the Baths of Sozius and found himself one among hundreds in the audience. It was hot. It was August sixteen hundred years ago and Strand was both in the Baths in the past and in the clock room in the present, and St. Augustine was both on the roof in the present and at the Baths in the past, where he had just vanquished Felix in debate, as he had vanquished Fortunatus before him, and Felix had just publicly recanted the error of the Manichean heresy which had been proven to him by the bishop's irrefutable reason. Felix returned to the church. Fortunatus had fled. Single-handedly, through the use of pure reason, St. Augustine had defeated the heretics and thus the heresy. Strand raised his hand to ask a question. It was an important question. But he could not catch the saint's eye.

"I never intended to stay in Syracuse," he said, and though no one in the crowd responded to his statement, it was still the truth. At twenty-four, two years before completing his doctorate, Strand had married. A year later his son John was born. When he finished his education he had a wife and a year old son and a daughter on the way. And not a job in sight. He applied for a job with a local corporation and was hired and that became Strand's life, though he had never planned it, could never have foreseen it, and was never happy with it. He stayed because the pay was good and he had a family to support. He settled in Syracuse and grew a pot belly.

"My boy was always restless," he said to the Christian seated alongside him, but the man's eyes were fast upon the stage where Felix was once again praising the bishop and the Church. Strand got up and walked away.

It was night and the woods felt darker and deeper than Strand remembered. All around him he could hear small life rustling through the undergrowth; above him things were moving in the trees. But before him he could see nothing but blackness. From behind he heard drums and primitive music, and he crawled on his stomach following the rhythm until he found himself at the edge of a circular clearing in the woods. In the center of the circle a campfire was burning. It was surrounded by men dressed in black robes, their heads covered with cowls.

"These are the Circumcellins," the Christian beside him whispered.

"The Circumcellins?" Strand asked.

"Heretics, fanatics, armed apostles of violence."

Strand nodded. At the edge of the circle there were amplifiers and electric guitars. On top of the amplifiers were canisters labelled: Cocaine, LSD, Angel Dust, Grass, Hash, Smack, Opium, Scotch, Bourbon, Whiskey, Mescaline, and many other words that Strand did not understand.

"John," Strand asked, "do you swear this was the only time? You never tried it before and you'll never try it again?"

The boy nodded, avoiding Strand's eyes. He was staring at a wall-sized poster of a man costumed as the devil, an electric guitar slung over his shoulder, a black tear painted falling from one eye.

Strand left the room crying and returned to the darkness of MONY Tower. On the roof above him St. Augustine was preaching to the city of Syracuse, but Strand was alone in the clock room, crying. He cried until he couldn't cry any longer. Then he climbed the last flight of stairs to the roof.

The wind was blowing hard and the saint didn't seem to notice Strand as he came alongside him and looked out over the city. People were gathered everywhere, straining to hear the saint speak. Cars were parked along Route 81 for as far as Strand could see, and people were standing on their cars staring at the tower. The waters of Onondaga Lake were filled with pleasure boats filled with passengers staring at the tower. People thronged to every window and rooftop, straining to hear St. Augustine's words.

But Strand, standing beside him, couldn't hear a thing, so he sat down at the saint's feet and closed his eyes, and he fell into darkness so deep he couldn't hear the beat of his heart or the sound of the blood in his veins, and he felt he had fallen at last into a void from which there was no hope of escape.

"*Tolle lege*," he heard the saint whisper.

Strand opened his eyes and found himself alone in his study. Though he had heard the saint's voice, he saw no one.

"Pick up and read," the saint repeated.

Strand did not question. He picked up the book in front of him and began reading. It was a difficult text full of deep and obscure passages, but Strand read intently and when there was something he absolutely could not understand, St. Augustine whispered the meaning in his ear with a voice like light and music, until Strand felt certain he was on the road to perfect knowledge, and soon, with the help of the bishop's reason, he would understand.

It was a sweet and peaceful feeling for Strand. He felt as though he were approaching the end of his struggle, as though, alone in his study within the city of Syracuse, he had found a special place, a place within a place, a city within a city.

PLATO
AT
SCRATCH
DANIEL'S

In 1944, when Danny was twenty, he met Hooper in a bombed-out basement in Cassino, Italy. The German-occupied town blocked the Allied advance to Rome, and for five months Danny had fought to take Cassino, suffering through a nightmarish winter of combat, a winter when he dreamed nightly of his own death. Then in May, when the battered town at last fell, he got cut off from his unit and found himself alone on a narrow cobblestone street, bracketed by the crumbling walls of what were once people's homes. He moved slowly. He crept along the street with his back pressed hard against a stone wall, the breech of his BAR snug against his heart and his left hand sweating tight around the hand guard. He took a short step and the wall behind him crumbled; and he fell backward onto a flight of stairs, tumbling several feet to a dark basement. When he sat up he saw Hooper sitting on a pile of rubble dressing a wound in his thigh.

"You all right?" Hooper asked.

Danny looked himself over. "Seem to be," he said. He nodded toward Hooper. "What about you?"

Hooper tied a strip of red cloth around his thigh in a bow. Blood was already soaking through it. He reached behind him and picked up half a broken bottle. It was streaked with blood. "Fell on this and gashed my leg," he said. He looked down at his shoes and shook his head and laughed quietly, as if he were remembering a private joke.

Danny laughed too. Hooper was a short man—five-six, five-seven at the most—whose most prominent feature was an extremely high forehead (there looked to be an inch and a half more space between his eyebrows and crown than was humanly possible), and he was skinny. He cut an amusing figure, laughing the way he was, sitting on a pile of broken stones in the semi-darkness with his pants down around his bony, pale legs and a red bandage decorating his slender thigh. So Danny laughed with Hooper while all around and above them the sharp, staccato claps of rapid gunfire echoed. "I just fell through the damn wall," he said, and they both laughed again. Then he noticed blood gathering in pools around the edge of Hooper's bandage and spilling in tiny rivulets down his leg. "Here. Let me help," he offered.

Hooper looked at the bandage and nodded. "You can't be any worse at this than I am."

Danny took two strips of linen from Hooper's first aid kit. After removing the blood-soaked bandage, he folded the first into a rectangular patch which he pressed hard against the wound until the bleeding stopped. Then he fastened the bandage tightly to the leg with the second trip.

Hooper thanked him and they shook hands; and as their hands met their eyes met too, and Danny felt awkward for a moment before turning and starting up the stairs. When he reached the top of the flight Hooper called to him from the basement shadows.

"By the way," he said, "where are you from?"

"Syracuse, New York," Danny answered, and from the darkness he heard Hooper's quiet laugh, and though he couldn't see him he knew he was looking at his feet and shaking his head as he laughed.

154

Thirty years later he saw Hooper again at Scratch Daniel's, a flashy, slick bar on the corner of East Onondaga and South Warren Streets in downtown Syracuse. The bar at Scratch Daniel's is some thirty feet long and behind it is a huge triptych of mirrors, the same as the bar in length and in height reaching from the floor to a twenty-foot ceiling. The barroom itself is narrow, the major part of it having been partitioned to serve as a dining room, and since the partition is mirrored with a triptych identical to the one behind the bar, a customer looking into either mirror can see his echoed image traveling forward and backward into a constantly shrinking infinity. This is precisely what Hooper was doing when Danny entered the bar on a quiet, snowy Syracuse afternoon: staring at his own image with wide and luminous eyes.

Only Hooper wasn't Hooper anymore. His skinny frame had been filled out with flesh and muscle so that he had to be described as stocky, and he wore a full, glistening gray beard over round, pudgy cheeks. His hair was shoulder-length and as gray as his beard, and he sat at the bar with a Greek toga draped over his clothes. He appeared rigid, seated on the bar stool, his eyes flashing as he stared at his own image. Thirty years had effected such changes in Hooper that Danny would have never recognized him if it weren't for the unmistakable forehead.

He considered introducing himself to Hooper, but the man appeared to be in a world of his own, so he took a seat at the opposite end of the bar and put a twenty dollar bill on the counter.

"What can I do you for?" the bartender asked. Like all the employees at Scratch Daniel's, the bartender was unusually good-looking and dressed in black shoes, black socks, black pants, black vest, and a white shirt.

"Scotch and water," Danny answered. As he watched the bartender go about preparing his drink, a pretty barmaid with long black hair came out of the kitchen and took some change from the cash register behind the bar. She nodded and smiled politely at Danny before returning to the kitchen. He wondered how the owners got away with hiring only beautiful people. There was something morally wrong, he suspected, with such a policy, but he came to Scratch Daniel's precisely because everything about the bar was clean, neat, and attractive, including the employees. "Listen," he said, lowering his voice when the bartender returned with his drink, "what's the story on that character in the toga?"

"That's Plato," the bartender replied, also lowering his voice. "He's harmless. Buy him an ouzo on the rocks and he'll do his number for you."

"What that?" Danny asked. "What number?"

The bartender smiled. "I promise he's harmless."

Danny pushed a five dollar bill forward on the counter.

"Plato," the bartender called. "This gentleman is offering you a drink."

For a moment Hooper's face turned solemn, but then he shook himself from whatever world he had been inhabiting and turned and looked at Danny.

In Hooper's eyes Danny saw not the least glimpse of recognition.

Hooper descended from his bar stool and joined Danny, pulling up a seat alongside him. The bartender, still smiling, set a glass with ice on the counter and covered the cubes with a clear liqueur which turned milky on contact with the ice.

Danny started to introduce himself to Hooper, but the bartender stopped him and spoke as if Hooper weren't there. "You just say *right*, or *yes*, or *true*, or something like that when he signals you. Otherwise he gets mad."

Danny nodded.

Hooper turned to Danny. "Tell me," he said, folding his hands and resting them in the lap of his toga, "what manner of government do you term oligarchy?" His voice was rich, deep, and authoritative.

Danny looked at the bartender. "Right," he said.

The bartender laughed.

Hooper looked at Danny sternly. "An oligarchy is a government resting on a valuation of property," he said, "in which the rich have power and the poor man is deprived of it."

Danny felt foolish. "Yes," he said. "I understand."

Hooper looked appeased by his response. "And tell me," he continued, "do you know what timocracy is?"

Danny shook his head.

"Government!" Hooper boomed, "in which love of honor is the ruling principle!"

"Right on!" the bartender said.

Danny laughed nervously.

"And how," Hooper asked, "does the change from timocracy to oligarchy arise?" He looked around the room as if awaiting an answer. Then he answered himself. "The accumulation of gold in the treasury of private individuals is the ruin of timocracy! They invent illegal modes of expenditure, for what do they or their wives care about the laws?" He looked at Danny, again awaiting a reply.

Danny was now entirely lost. When the bartender nudged him he said, "Yes. Right."

"Yes indeed!" Hooper said, and put one hand on Danny's shoulder. "And then one, seeing another grow rich, seeks to rival him, and thus the great mass of citizens becomes lovers of money."

"That's true," Danny said.

"The gospel," the bartender added.

"And so they grow richer and richer, and the more they think of making a fortune the less they think of virtue, for when riches and virtue are placed together in the scales of balance, the one always rises as the other falls."

"Amen!" the bartender said.

Danny laughed. "It's the truth," he said.

"And in proportion as riches and rich men are honored in the State, virtue and the virtuous are dishonored."

"Right," Danny said.

"Right," the bartender said.

"And what is honored is cultivated, and that which has no honor is neglected."

"Hallelujah!" the bartender said.

"And so at last, instead of loving contention and glory, men become lovers of trade and money. They honor and look up to the rich man, and make a ruler of him, and dishonor the poor man."

"They do," Danny said, and by then he was listening carefully to Hooper and for the next hour he and the bartender—whose name he learned was Allie—listened to Hooper discourse on the nature of good and bad government. Danny was engrossed in the talk, and Allie, who had heard parts of it before and occasionally walked away to tend to some business, also seemed interested.

When it was all over, Hooper indicated with a nod that his one-sided dialogue had come to an end. The bartender applauded, and Danny wanted to shake his hand, but he had hopped quickly from the bar stool, pulling the toga over his head as he approached the coatrack near the entrance to the bar, and before Danny could figure out what he wanted to say, Hooper had stuffed the toga inside his coat and was on his way out the door.

"Hooper!" Danny called. "Wait a second!"

In the half-opened doorway, framed in part by the darkness of the bar and in part by the white snow falling behind him, Hooper turned slowly around, his face screwed up into a grimace, his lips pulled back in a snarl revealing yellow teeth locked savagely together.

Allie took a step backward, and Danny took a firm hold on the molding of the bar. Hooper hesitated in the doorway, and then turned and walked out into the light and snow.

"Jesus Holy Christ!" Allie said. "What in God's name did you say to him?"

Danny shook himself sharply, as if reacting to a chill. "That was unbelievable," he said. "I thought he was going to attack us."

"What's this *Hooper?*" Allie asked.

"That's his name. We were in Italy together in the war."

"The war?" Allie said. "World War Two?"

Danny looked at him as if he were crazy. Of course World War Two. Then he realized how young Allie was, probably at the beginning of his twenties, and that World War Two, for him, was something he had only read about. He nodded. "World War Two," he said. "We saw combat together in Italy."

"Jesus," he said. "Plato's a war buddy of yours and his real name is Hooper." He said this factually, as if straightening things out for his own understanding.

"I wouldn't call him a war buddy," Danny said. "I met him when we took Cassino. I don't even know his first name. He had Hooper stenciled on his uniform."

158

"He's Plato to us," Allie said.

"I can see."

"He's a Hutchings' patient. He's been coming around for a year or so. A shrink I know says he spends all his time reading. You know, he wasn't making that stuff up."

"He wasn't?" Danny said.

Allie shook his head. "It's from *The Republic,* by Plato. The real Plato. He's memorized the whole damn thing."

Danny looked surprised.

"Here," Allie said. He reached under the cash register and took out a paperback copy of *The Republic.* "I keep this around for the skeptics. I don't know what part it is," he handed the book to Danny, "but if you look through it you'll find everything he was saying."

Danny held the book in his hand. It was impressive feeling. "He's memorized this whole thing?"

Allie nodded. "It's how he makes spending money. He goes around to different bars in the day—anyplace within walking distance of Hutchings—and he usually finds someone and they buy him drinks and sometimes slip a few bucks into his coat pocket when they leave. He's got a following."

Danny laughed. "That's amazing," he said. "What a character."

"No shit," Allie said. "And you say his name is Hooper and he and you were in World War Two together. What was it like, the war?"

Danny looked down at the bar and thought about the question. He shrugged. "What's to say?" He took a five dollar bill out of his wallet, pushed it across the counter, and started for the door.

"This a tip?" Allie asked, surprised.

Danny nodded. "You been good company."

"Well, hot damn!" Allie said, affecting a country-Southern accent. "Y'all come on back soon now. Ya hear?"

"Will do," Danny answered, and he gave a little half-wave as he walked out of the bar into the snow.

His truck was parked in the municipal lot alongside the court house and by the time he got to it, the snow had stopped falling. He nudged the truck out onto the street and twenty minutes later was out of the city and following a series of winding roads to Bale Road on Onondaga Lake in Liverpool, where he lived alone in a house built to accommodate a medium-sized family.

He pulled the truck to a stop in front of his attached studio (which used to be a garage before he bought the house and had it converted); and, getting out, he walked around to the back door, which he kept unlocked. Behind him he could hear the water of Onondaga Lake slapping against the shore. He walked quickly through a meticulously neat and well-furnished living room and through an equally clean kitchen to his studio. The studio door had two big locks on it: a mortise and a rim lock. It looked like the door to a vault stuck in the middle of someone's kitchen. Danny wasn't fond of the locks, but he earned his living by restoring paintings, and since he sometimes spent months working on paintings worth a great deal of money, he needed the extra security.

Currently he was doing an extensive cleanup for the Everson Museum. They had managed to acquire, with the aid of a big publicity campaign and donation drive, Edward Hicks's *The Peaceable Kingdom* and had engaged him to work on it before its initial exhibition. He reached up to the cabinet alongside the refrigerator, pushed a box of Cheerios aside, and turned off the burglar alarm. Then he released first the higher rim lock and then the mortise lock. Inside the studio, Hicks's painting rested on an easel in the center of the room, and the late afternoon light coming through the studio's barred windows cast the shadows of the bars over the surface of the painting so that the painting itself looked to be behind bars.

Danny lifted the easel and turned it to face the lake-side light, illuminating the painting with a steadier, if dimmer light. He had had the painting for a couple of weeks and was coming to like it a great deal, better than either Bingham's *Fur Traders on the Missouri* or Homer's *Breezing Up,* two other well-known American paintings he particularly admired. There was something special about this painting by a Pennsylvania preacher and sign painter who was attempting, simply, to make apparent the Word of God. The Prophet Isaiah said, "The wolf shall dwell with the lamb, and the leopard shall lie down with the kid, and the lion shall eat straw like the ox," and so Hicks painted just such a peaceful menagerie and threw in, for good measure, William Penn signing his peace treaty with the Indians. But it was the animals and children in the foreground of the painting that most impressed Danny, the way the eyes of the cats seemed transfixed, as though they were staring outward at the viewer, awaiting a sign, and the way the children seemed so carefully posed—and so ugly. There was something about it all that fascinated him. He pulled up a chair alongside the window and studied the painting awhile longer, but meeting Hooper again after so many years had stirred up uncomfortable feelings, and he turned and looked out through the bars at the snow falling over Onondaga Lake. The surface of the water was dull gray, and where the wind ran across it, choppy and white with foam. What had happened between then and now? he asked himself. Between meeting Hooper in a bombed-out basement in Italy and meeting him again in a bar in Syracuse? He thought about the question and couldn't find anything of singular importance. He had none of the conventional milestones by which others measure their lives. He had never married, nor had any children. He had never even been in love, though there had been women in his life, even some who claimed to love him. Both his parents were still alive, as were two younger brothers, though he hardly saw them since his brothers married and left Syracuse and his parents retired to Florida. Aside from his work and his music—he studied and played flute—there wasn't a lot to Danny's life, and though this hadn't bothered him before, seeing Hooper made him think about the passing time, and thinking about it disturbed him.

He considered working on the painting, but decided, instead, in order to cheer himself up, to make a big meal. He locked the studio and started to work on a spaghetti-and-meatball dinner, but instead of getting involved in the cooking, as he usually did, he found himself performing each task mechanically. Hooper's recitation of Plato's dialogue had resurrected an odd memory. After the war he had spent a few weeks at an army base in Kentucky, before being honorably discharged and sent home. One Sunday morning he had awakened wanting to go to church, though he hadn't been since he was a child. He got dressed and outside the barracks met a group of black recruits on their way to services. They were embarrassed but they let him join them, and he wound up in a small country church, the only white face in an all black congregation. He hadn't thought about that Sunday in thirty years, but now he remembered clearly a huge black preacher looming over a dwarfed pulpit, and he remembered the words he bellowed in a sonorous, forbidding music: "Greed and violence, brothers and sisters! Greed and violence!" Though he couldn't remember anything else from the service, those words the preacher shouted, accusing, were sharp and clear, and they repeated themselves annoyingly in Danny's mind, over and over. By the time the meal was cooked and set on the dining room table, he was feeling surly and mean.

"I can't believe this," he said, and slapped his fork down on the table. He shook his head and looked around him, and when he found himself for the first time in a very long time feeling something like fear at the silence and emptiness of his house, he stood up and got his hat and coat out of the hall closet. He left his dinner on the table, and took the truck into the city.

At the Harrison-Adams exit he got off Route 81, but instead of turning right on Harrison and heading into the city, as he had thought he would do, he turned left on Adams and drove to Hutchings.

"I can't believe this," he said again as he drove into the parking lot, but he followed his impulse through. After having some trouble finding the right entrance, he walked up to a woman dressed in a doctor's white coat who was seated behind a metal desk.

"Excuse me," he said. "I'd like to visit a patient by the name of Hooper."

The woman looked concerned. She checked the time on her wristwatch and then, as if to be absolutely sure she wasn't confused, looked up at the large institutional clock hanging on the wall behind her. "It's well past visiting hours," she said. "Is there something wrong?"

Danny stared at her. He felt strange and disoriented and wasn't sure what he should say. He put his hands in his pockets. "He's a friend of mine from the war," he said. "We were there when they took Cassino. He was wounded and—"

"Just a moment, sir." She put her hand up to signal him to wait a second. She picked up the black phone on her desk, pressed a button and dialed a number. "Doctor Hammer to the front desk, please," she said politely. Then she smiled at Danny and hung up.

"Oh shit," Danny said. "God damn." He turned and started for the door.

"Sir!" she called after him. "Sir!"

But Danny was already out the door and jogging through the parking lot to his truck. After he started it up, he sat behind the wheel and watched. At the entrance to the hospital, two men joined the woman at the door, and all three of them stared at Danny's truck and talked among themselves. When one of the men finally stepped outside, Danny put the truck in gear and headed home.

For the rest of that winter he tried not to think about Hooper, and avoided going to any bars where he might run into him. Hooper made him question his life. When he started thinking about Hooper he wound up thinking of himself, thinking he had never married or had children, thinking he had not accomplished anything of value with his life; and such a bleak appraisal of his life depressed him. He spent the winter working around the house, restoring little-known paintings, and trying to improve himself as a flutist. He put Hooper out of mind as best he could. But in the spring, after Onondaga Lake had gone through its annual freeze and thaw, something happened in a department store in downtown Syracuse.

He was shopping for a jogging suit when he heard the unmistakable sound of gunshots coming from the floor above him. For a moment or two after the gunfire, the store was so quiet that Danny could hear the electronic hum of hundreds of cash registers. Then there was panic. People came charging down the escalator, rushing for the exits, and shoppers screamed for lost friends and missing children. From the top of the escalator a thin woman called for a doctor, then collapsed against the balustrade and was carried slowly to the first floor landing.

Danny's instincts told him to leave, but he was relatively

calm and stood his ground, and eventually, because he decided it was the right thing to do, he went up to the second floor to see if he could help. The store had turned quiet again, and as Danny stepped off the stairs he saw a handful of people milling around the furniture department. One man, a few feet away in the appliance department, was sitting on a stove: his feet dangled a few inches above the floor as he violently rubbed his temples with his fingertips. Beyond him, Danny saw a man lying on a fourposter bed, his open eyes staring up at the bright fabric of the canopy, and as he moved closer he saw a dark stain of blood under the man's head soaking through the quilt and into the partially exposed pillows. He moved even closer and saw that part of the base of the man's head was missing where the bullet must have exited. At the foot of the bed, half covered by the side curtains, he saw a bright silver automatic pistol.

The man was a stranger to Danny, but he approached until he was close enough to touch him, and when he finally stopped, he shook his head half in disgust and half in sorrow. Then he saw the others: the woman kneeling over a coffee table, her torso resting on the slick mahogany surface, and the two small children who looked to be sleeping comfortably on the wide cushions of an expensive sofa, red stains soaking ugly circles through the fabric of their matching white jackets. He turned his back on the scene and saw a small group of onlookers.

"It's a tragedy," one of the people said as Danny approached them.

"I knew him," another said. "They were buying furniture for their new house. "That's his wife and children."

But Danny wasn't listening. With the scream of approaching sirens in the background, he took the escalator down to the first floor and headed for the street. Outside, none of the hundreds of people busy traversing the streets seemed aware of the tragedy that had just taken place so close to them. Danny watched them scurry against a background of bright steel and glass, and it looked as though every one of them were in the midst of doing something important. They didn't look at each other. They all walked quickly, their eyes set on a distant goal.

Danny turned and headed for Scratch Daniel's. With a little luck, he thought, he might find Hooper there. If not, he could always check the other local bars, and in time he'd find him. And this time, he decided, he'd be careful not to call him Hooper. "If he wants to be Plato," Danny said aloud, "Plato he is." Alongside him, an attractive young girl dressed smartly in a navy-blue business suit heard him talking to himself and looked at him as if he were diseased. Danny noticed. He turned and scowled at her and then hurried down the street to the bar, feeling, suddenly, as if he had an appointment of some importance.